Beth wondered if Matt would come back...

Although she'd planned to be long gone by the time Matt O'Malley showed up this morning, things hadn't gone according to plan. Sarah had kept her up most of the night, alternately crying and feeding. Now here she was, feeling like death warmed over and still at the hospital. She was in no state to head back to the cabin and try to manage Sarah while she was so exhausted. It wouldn't hurt to stay another day, as long as Matt didn't press her for any more answers to his questions.

She was happy Matt had turned up today. When she'd seen him standing there looking so dependable, his eyes full of compassion, Beth had felt warmth and gratitude down to her toes.

Careful! a little voice warned. *It isn't smart to rely on Matt O'Malley. He's a cop.*

Dear Reader,

The Sheriff and the Baby is my second novel for Harlequin American Romance and also the second in the O'Malley Men series.

Those of you who met Matt, the long-suffering, law-abiding brother of my hero in *Colorado Christmas*, were curious to know if he finds love again, after mourning his wife for so many years.

Matt is now the county sheriff and in this "opposites attract" story, he has to choose between love and duty when he falls for a damsel in distress who turns out to be a fugitive from the law.

I've been delighted to receive so much reader mail about my debut novel, *Colorado Christmas*, and fascinated to discover how different aspects of that story affected readers. Many enjoyed the antics of Louella—particularly my husband, who asked if she'd be a continuing character in the series.

I hope you'll enjoy *The Sheriff and the Baby* and watch out for the return of Louella in a small (nonspeaking) part!

Extras about the book, like the people I modeled the characters on and the town that inspired the O'Malley Men series, can be found on my Web site: www.cccoburn.com or you can write to me at cc@cccoburn.com. I'd love to hear from you.

And please watch for the third O'Malley Men story, *Colorado Cowboy*, to see how oldest brother, Luke—the taciturn rancher—copes with learning he has a fourteen-year-old son. *Colorado Cowboy* is coming in October.

Happy reading! Healthy lives!

C.C. Coburn

The Sheriff and the Baby

C.C. COBURN

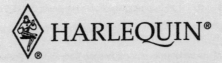

HARLEQUIN®

TORONTO • NEW YORK • LONDON
AMSTERDAM • PARIS • SYDNEY • HAMBURG
STOCKHOLM • ATHENS • TOKYO • MILAN • MADRID
PRAGUE • WARSAW • BUDAPEST • AUCKLAND

Recycling programs
for this product may
not exist in your area.

ISBN-13: 978-0-373-75313-0

THE SHERIFF AND THE BABY

This edition published by arrangement with Harlequin Books S.A.

For questions and comments about the quality of this book
please contact us at Customer_eCare@Harlequin.ca

www.eHarlequin.com

Printed in U.S.A.

ABOUT THE AUTHOR

C.C. Coburn married the first man who asked her and hasn't regretted a day since—well, not many of them! She grew up in Australia's Outback, moved to its sun-drenched Pacific coast, then traveled the world. A keen skier, she discovered Colorado's majestic Rocky Mountains and now divides her time between Australia and Colorado. Home will always be Australia, where she lives with her husband, three grown children, a Labrador and three cats—but her heart and soul are also firmly planted in Colorado. She loves hearing from readers. You can visit her at www.cccoburn.com.

Books by C.C. Coburn

HARLEQUIN AMERICAN ROMANCE
1283—COLORADO CHRISTMAS

Acknowledgments

I'm indebted to Sheriff John Minor of Summit County, Colorado, for his invaluable help with police procedures. Any omissions or mistakes are entirely the fault of the author (and her imagination).

Many thanks to midwife and fellow author Fiona Lowe for helping me with all things maternity. And to Gary Nicholds, former hospital administrator for his assistance with hospital regulations and procedures.

My editor, Paula Eykelhof, who in her quietly spoken Canadian accent, patiently explained that it wouldn't be possible for the sheriff to nurse the baby or to wrap a baby in a rug! As always, she's alert to the different meanings and nuances between Australian and North American English and customs, and I thank her for that.

And although I always thank him last, he comes first in my life—my husband, Keith, best friend, supporter and fan. I'm happy to report that he's finally read one of my books (and better still, enjoyed it).

Chapter One

Blinding snow blew horizontally across the deserted road, blasting against the side of Sheriff Matt O'Malley's SUV. He swore as his headlights picked out the red sports car swerving ahead of him and hit the siren, warning the driver to slow down.

Judging by the California license plates, it was probably college kids on spring break. Rich city kids foolhardy enough to think they were capable of driving in the extreme winter conditions of the Colorado Rockies.

He gripped his wheel as the smaller car swerved into the path of an oncoming vehicle. Caught in the glare of its headlights, the sports car's driver turned sharply off the road and went over an embankment.

Veering to miss it, the oncoming vehicle swung onto Matt's side of the road. He spun his wheel, fighting the momentum of his powerful Ford Excursion and the road's slippery surface as the other vehicle missed him by inches and continued into the night.

Cold sweat trickled down his back as he pulled over and leaped out. The sports car's headlights reflected back eerily through the snow, its horn blaring. Matt tore open the door and shone his flashlight inside.

The only occupant was the driver, a young woman, slumped over the wheel. Fingers shaking, he checked her pulse and released his breath when he detected it beating strongly against his fingertips.

She moaned and lifted her head.

"Careful," he said, easing her away from the steering wheel and collapsed air bag. The horn stopped blaring and she opened her eyes but her gaze was unfocused. Although her face was pale, there was no smell of alcohol on her breath nor any sign of blood—thankfully.

Matt returned to his vehicle and radioed the county communication center. "This is Command One," he barked, trying to keep the panic out of his voice. "I need an ambulance at my location. Highway 5, four miles south of Silver Springs."

"I'm sorry, Sheriff," the operator said. "But one of our rigs just went off the road at the pass and now we've got calls backed up all over the place. It'll be at least an hour before we can get there."

Matt cursed and broke the connection, grabbed some blankets and hurried back to the woman. "It's okay, ma'am. The ambulance is on its way," he assured her. Hating the lie. Hating winter as he tucked the blankets around her.

She moaned again, then braced her hands on the steering wheel and screamed.

Matt's blood froze at the sound. Had she sustained internal injuries? His limited first-aid training was no match for the woman's agony as she gripped the steering wheel so hard her knuckles turned white.

He hunkered down beside her. "Can you tell me where it hurts?"

"My baby!" Panting so rapidly she was beyond speech, she gripped Matt's hand, drew it inside her bulky coat and placed it on her stomach.

Matt stared, horrified. The bulging, rigidly taut stomach beneath his hand didn't fit with her slim features. Lord knew what sort of injuries both she and her child might have sustained.

Please, not again, he begged as memories threatened to overwhelm him. He waited as she breathed through the contraction, his hand resting on her belly as though he could impart some of his strength to her.

Finally, he felt the contraction's intensity subsiding as her stomach softened beneath his touch. She turned scared gray eyes to his and said, "I need to get…to the hospital. *Now.*"

Matt didn't want to move her. Didn't want to be responsible for this woman. The memories flooded back, threatening to drown him, but he couldn't afford the luxury of self-pity. Not now.

"You could have other injuries, ma'am. I'll put through another call to the ambulance…tell them how urgent it is."

He was about to return to his vehicle, but she grabbed his arm. "No time," she panted, her eyes squeezed tightly closed against the worst of the pain. "Water broke…contractions…too close…together… You take—" Her last words became a howl of agony as she threw back her head and half cried, half panted.

A hot poker twisted in Matt's guts. Had it been like this for Sally? Alone, afraid, in terrible pain? It had happened three years ago and he still couldn't forgive himself, couldn't forget.

"Please…please help me," she sobbed as tears squeezed from the corners of her eyes and ran down her cheeks. "Please?"

He cursed the ambulance that'd run off the road and left him with the responsibility of this woman and her child. The heat burned in his gut as memories forced their way to the surface. As they receded, he reached in, unclipped her seat belt and lifted her into his arms.

Praying she wasn't injured internally, he uttered the words meant to reassure a trauma victim. "It's okay, ma'am. I'll take care of you. Everything'll be fine." *As long as you hold off giving birth until I can get you to the hospital…*

After placing her on his passenger seat, he fastened the seat belt around her. "We'll be there soon," he said, climbing into the driver's seat. He was headed down the highway toward the hospital in Silver Springs before he fastened his own seat belt. That done, he glanced over at her. She was slumped against the seat back, her eyes closed. Fearing he might have damaged something in his desperation to get her to the hospital, he asked, "Ma'am? Are you okay?"

She opened her eyes and looked around, disoriented.

"I'm going to call ahead to the hospital to let them know you're coming," he explained. "Can you give me your name?"

She hesitated, confusion and fear chasing across her features. Then she leaned forward, gripped the dashboard with both hands and screamed.

Horrified, Matt swerved to miss a car as it loomed out of the snowstorm.

He put a call through to the county hospital in Silver Springs. The nurse in Maternity promptly grasped the situation when she heard the young woman screaming. "I can't hear you!" he yelled. "Can you repeat?"

"There's no need to shout, Sheriff O'Malley," she said as the young woman's cries of pain became less strident. "What's the patient's name?"

He looked across at her and asked, "What's your name?"

"Beth, um…" Her brow furrowed as though she had trouble remembering.

"Ma'am?" Matt prompted when she hesitated again.

"It's Beth…" She raised pain-filled eyes to his, then glanced at the steering wheel. "Ford," she breathed through the last of the contraction, then rested her head against the seat back and closed her eyes. "Beth Ford," she repeated.

Matt frowned at the insignia in the center of his steering wheel and resisted the urge to challenge her. Instead, he relayed the information.

"How far apart are her contractions?"

How much more personal could this get? Beth Ford was panting again, her face contorted with pain. "How the hell do I know! She's starting to have another one, if that's any help."

"And her due date?"

"What's with all the questions? The kid's coming *now!* I can't tell it to stop," he yelled, feeling himself losing control and hating it.

"Do you wish to pull over and deliver the child?" came the disembodied voice.

Finally his control snapped. "Are you *crazy?* Of course not! Just get everything ready. I'll be there in two minutes. And, by the way, she's been in an MVA."

Matt cut the connection and concentrated on the road. It was hard enough driving on snow-covered roads at high speed. It was something else again to do it with a woman screaming at the top of her lungs.

"Would you like me to contact your husband?" he offered.

"No…no husband," she said, then looked out the window, her lips pressed tightly together.

Matt didn't miss the sheen of tears seconds before she'd turned away. "Anyone else you want me to contact?"

She shook her head. "No. No one. I'm…a widow."

Yeah, right. And I'm Santa Claus. There was no disgrace

in single motherhood. Why couldn't people be honest about it?

Strange, the way she'd come up with the name emblazoned on the wheel of his Ford Excursion. Even stranger that there was no one he could contact for her. Everybody had someone, didn't they?

"Okay, fine," he muttered and sped through the Silver Springs town limits. Some of the tension in his shoulders eased as the hospital loomed ahead on the right. He'd made it. He could hand her over to people who knew what to do with screaming women and impatient babies.

He pulled up at the hospital's emergency room entrance. A medical team with a gurney waited just inside the doors.

Matt was out and opening his passenger's door before the team had even emerged from the sheltering warmth of the hospital.

"Everything's going to be okay," he said as much to reassure himself as her. "These folks will take real good care of you and your baby."

Recognizing several members of the team, Matt nodded to them as they took charge. In spite of being surrounded by people with the expertise to care for pregnant women, Matt felt a strange reluctance to relinquish his responsibility to her. What if something went wrong? Who would protect her? Beth Ford apparently had no one.

The doors whooshed open again and his spirits lifted when Dr. Lucy Cochrane, an old school friend, strode up to the gurney. She spoke quietly to Beth, then turned to him. "She'll be fine, Matt." Lucy clasped his hands in hers. She looked into his eyes, but he glanced away, afraid of what she might see there, and hating the pity he could read in hers. Like everyone in Spruce Lake, Lucy knew how he'd failed his wife when she'd needed him most. If he'd gone straight home that evening three years ago, Sally might still be alive.

"She'll be fine, Matt," Lucy told him again. "You've done well."

Too choked with emotion to answer, he was about to step inside to grab a cup of coffee when he felt Beth Ford's hand clasp his.

She looked scared stiff and her hand trembled in his. Her eyes closed tightly for a moment as she fought to control the pain. When she opened them, Matt's heart constricted. He'd never seen anyone look so afraid, so alone, in his life. "Stay with me. Please?" she begged softly.

MATT STOOD BESIDE HER BED in the delivery room, Beth Ford's hand in his. They'd been there barely five minutes and he'd lost count of the number of times she'd crushed his hand with each contraction. Sure that in a minute or so his hand would be pulp, he eased it from her and replaced it with the other, then flexed his fingers.

The lighthearted banter of the delivery-room team seemed to have a calming effect on their patient. At least she wasn't screaming anymore. Maybe that was why you were supposed to have a coach—someone to take over the thinking for you. Sure as hell you wouldn't be able to think straight when you were in so much pain.

Lucy couldn't resist a few cracks about his squeamishness, telling the patient she was lucky they'd made it to the hospital. He forced himself to grin and bear the jokes at his expense.

When Beth cried out as another contraction hit, Matt suggested, trying to keep the panic from his voice, that they give her painkillers.

"Too late," came Lucy's clipped reply. "Here comes the head. Do you want to look?"

Matt almost passed out.

With a skill obviously born of long practice, the male nurse wheeled a stool beneath Matt with his foot while helping Lucy at the other end of the delivery bed. "Sit," he ordered curtly, then in soothing tones, went back to telling Beth how and when to pant.

Matt stared at the wall in front of him, trying to focus on something, anything, other than the need to get up and run—or fall off the stool in a dead faint.

Suddenly this slippery-looking thing was placed on Beth's chest and she was crying and laughing all at once.

"You've got a beautiful baby girl," Lucy announced.

It didn't look much like a baby to Matt, kind of wrinkled and red and covered in white stuff and—his stomach churned—*blood*.

He tried to stand but his legs felt wobbly. He sat down again and stared at the wall some more and took deep breaths to ward off the light-headedness.

"Thank you," Beth whispered, and he turned to look at her. Her faced glowed. Gone was the pain and the fear in her eyes. She was…radiant.

"I couldn't have done it without you," she murmured, her eyes filling with tears.

Matt couldn't speak. His throat had dried up and his tongue was glued to the roof of his mouth.

"What's your mother's name?" she asked.

"Why?" he choked.

"I'd like to name my daughter after her."

"That isn't necessary."

"I don't suppose you want to cut the cord?" Lucy interrupted.

Matt glared at her. He cleared his throat and asked Beth, "Why not name her after your own mom?"

A shadow of pain skittered across her features. "I…I

can't do that." She expelled a sigh full of anguish. "It would mean a lot to me if I could name her after your mom."

When Matt hesitated, she offered him a tiny smile and said, "She gave birth to someone who helped me when I needed it most."

What the hell? He was never going to see Beth Ford again. What harm could it do? "Sarah. With an *h*."

She smoothed her hand over the infant's head in a protective gesture. "Hi, Sarah. Welcome to the world," she said and placed a kiss on her daughter's forehead.

Matt swallowed. Beth Ford should be sharing this moment with someone she was close to, not a stranger.

Not someone as undeserving as him.

He fought the bile rising in his throat. "Are you sure there isn't someone I can contact for you?" he asked.

She shook her head and looked away.

She was fighting tears again. Matt's heart went out to her. If she was a widow, then surely a relative could be with her instead? A friend? She needed *someone*. Someone more worthy than him.

Eventually she glanced back at him. "There's…no one. But thank you." She held the baby closer. "There's just the two of us now," she whispered, but he noticed the trembling in her hand.

Matt's instincts told him something wasn't right here. Beth was afraid of something, why else would she have given him a false name? Was she on the run from an abusive husband? Was that why she'd claimed she was a widow?

Lucy's voice broke into his thoughts as she addressed Beth. "The nurse is going to take your baby for a few minutes to weigh her and check that everything's okay while I deliver the placenta."

That did it! Matt launched himself off the stool and

walked into the corridor with as much dignity and speed as he could manage.

He leaned against the cool wall, sucked in several deep breaths, then slid down and put his head between his knees. He'd never felt so exhausted, bewildered or overwhelmed in his life. Thank God he wasn't wearing his uniform. Wouldn't do for members of the public to see the sheriff half passed out in a hospital corridor.

Matt was relieved he'd made it to the hospital. The thought of trying to handle everything he'd just witnessed by himself was too terrifying to contemplate. How the staff stayed so cool, calm and collected while their patient howled with pain… He shook his head.

After a few minutes he'd recovered his equilibrium and stood. He headed to his vehicle and radioed the state patrol to ask them for an accident investigation and have Hank Farquar tow Beth's car.

Bone-weary with exhaustion, he went home for some much-needed sleep.

Tomorrow, he'd find out exactly why the woman with the anxious gray eyes was lying to him.

Chapter Two

When his alarm woke him at seven. Matt lay in bed, staring up at the ceiling, and thought about Beth Ford and her tiny baby.

He smiled. *Sarah*. His mom would be tickled to know a scared young woman had valued his efforts enough to name a baby in her honor.

His cat, Wendy—one of his nieces had gone through a fascination with *The Adventures of Peter Pan*—settled on his chest and purred loudly. Soon she'd poke her claws in his comforter, informing him that it was time for breakfast. This usually went on for five minutes while Matt talked himself into getting out of bed.

But this morning, he felt a sense of elation and even anticipation and couldn't wait to get started on his day. For the first time in three years, he hadn't woken with a burning in his gut that threatened to tear him apart.

He called the hospital and was assured that Beth and her baby had had a comfortable night. Maybe he should drop in before work to check on them, just to make sure. His abrupt departure the night before must've made her think he was an imbecile.

He moved around his tiny apartment in the early-morning darkness. *Convenient* was about the only thing he could say in its favor. He'd taken over the apartment above the florist shop when his brother, Will, had married Becky McBride, the town judge. Soon he'd start building a home among the spruce and pines on his ten-acre lot in another valley.

Even the prospect of building his home hadn't completely lifted the melancholy that had been his unwanted companion for too long. But this morning he was looking forward to beginning work on his house, to sharing the building of his home with his brothers. Their father, Mac, would give them all the benefit of his wisdom whether they wanted it or not, while his mom and sister-in-law, Becky, would keep the workers well-fed. He smiled at the thought of them all working together. Family was everything to Matt.

Was that why he hadn't been eager to build his home until now—because he didn't have a family of his own? He pictured a woman who looked like Beth leaning against the kitchen counter, smiling up at him, a baby perched on her hip.

This was crazy! He needed coffee to clear his head, and lots of it.

He hurried to the tiny kitchen and cursed when he stubbed his toe on a piece of cedar furniture that was too big for the apartment but would be perfect for his new home. Then he tripped over Wendy as she wound her way around his legs.

His cell rang. Matt snatched it up and tipped kibble into Wendy's dish. She rewarded him by rubbing against his leg and purring loudly.

"Hey, little brother," came the booming voice of his oldest brother, Luke, who ran the family ranch. "I hear you had a busy night rescuing damsels in distress."

Matt cursed and poured himself a coffee; thankfully it was ready, since it had been set to brew when his alarm went off. News traveled too fast in Peaks County. You couldn't scratch yourself without someone ten miles down the valley hearing about it.

He took a gulp of coffee and asked, "How'd you hear?"

"Hank, of course."

Matt shook his head. There wasn't anything Hank, the tow-truck operator, universal busybody and cousin of Mayor Frank Farquar, didn't know and wouldn't pass on to anyone who'd listen.

"What did Hank say?"

"Didn't get it from Hank. Heard it through his cousin, Chuck, who told one of the guys down at the feed store."

Frustrated, Matt raked a hand through his hair. Hank's gossiping was out of control. One day he was going to tell the wrong person the wrong thing and someone would end up getting hurt. "What *exactly* did you hear?" he demanded in as patient a tone as he could manage.

"Correct me if I'm wrong," Luke cautioned, although he was as aware of Hank's inability to get the facts straight as Matt was. "He got a call to tow a little red sports car that had been driven into a snowbank off the highway."

So far, so good. "Go on."

"According to Hank, the driver had a baby right there in the front seat and you delivered it!"

Matt squirmed. His weak stomach was legend in the family. As a kid on the ranch, he'd always made himself scarce when calves needed birthing, castration or branding. Teasing Matt over his aversion to blood had been his big brother's way of getting under his skin ever since they were kids. It worked, too. Only this time, he'd overstepped his bounds.

Luke's guffaws died away. "Ah, jeez…I'm sorry, Matt. I didn't think…" he apologized. "Sally—"

"Forget it," Matt cut in, not wanting to let his personal tragedy intrude. The morning was too promising to dwell on the past.

While it was appealing to play the hero regarding the events of the night before, Matt knew that soon enough the truth would get out and come back to haunt him. "We made it to the hospital." he said, reaching for a can of cat food. Wendy was in full hurry-up-I'm-starvin'-to-death mode, even though her bowl of kibble had been licked clean.

"And you stayed for the birth?" Luke pressed.

Matt cleared his throat. "Ah, yeah." He ripped the lid off the can and spooned some cat food into Wendy's bowl. Predictably, she leaped on it.

"Hot damn! Did you pass out?"

Matt could feel his hackles rising. "No, I did not," he said with as much dignity as he could muster. "Look, I've got to go. If you don't have anything more pressing to talk about, I'll catch you later."

"Hang on. You haven't told me whether the baby was a boy or a girl or anything about the mom. And what about the father? Where was he?"

Matt couldn't believe this. His normally reserved brother had all of a sudden turned chatty.

"A girl. And she's a widow," he answered shortly. His stomach was grumbling and a plate of ham and eggs with four helpings of Texas toast from Rusty's Grill looked mighty tempting. Hell, even Wendy's breakfast was starting to look tempting.

It took Luke a moment to register the curtly delivered information. "She's a widow?" he asked. "Poor thing. And a daughter, you say? That's nice."

Matt could hear the softening in his brother's voice. Luke was partial to daughters, seeing as he had three of them.

"So was she here on holiday?"

"What is this, twenty questions?" Matt was getting grumpy. The coffee had worn off and his stomach was growling. "I have no idea. She doesn't seem to know anyone."

"Sounds mysterious. Now, why would a woman who's about to have a baby be traveling alone?"

Matt had wondered the same thing. The woman *was* a mystery. Why was she in this part of Colorado without any support? "I have no idea," he said again. "She was in no condition to answer questions last night, but I'm going to stop by the hospital. I've got to get some details for my report," he explained, not wanting Luke to infer that he had anything other than a professional interest in the woman, "so maybe I'll find out something then."

"And you'll get back to me?" Luke asked.

"In your dreams. She and her daughter deserve some privacy. And I think you'd do well to ignore Hank's gossiping."

"Oh?" Luke sounded put out. "Well, gotta go," he said and rang off.

Relieved that his brother had found something more interesting to do than chew the fat with him, Matt grabbed his coat and headed down to Rusty's.

BETH STRETCHED HER ARMS above her head. In spite of being woken just after 4:00 a.m. to feed Sarah, she'd had her best night's sleep in four months. The only decent one since Marcus was killed. She closed her eyes against the painful memories. Time enough to deal with those. Right now, she was starting on a new phase of her life.

A nurse stuck her head around the door and grinned. "You're awake! I've got someone who wants to see you," she said. "I'll be right back."

Beth stared after her, bewildered. No one knew she was here—except the guy who'd brought her in last night.

A vague memory surfaced. Tall. *Very* tall…and good-looking. Even through the pain, she'd noticed his features—neatly trimmed dark brown hair, broad shoulders, a strong jaw and intense dark brown eyes. *Eyes that wouldn't let you hide many secrets.*

She shivered, wondering where that notion had come from. Was it because she had so many secrets and was terrified of being caught out? Lying didn't come easily to her. But she'd needed to lie to the stranger—to protect herself and especially her baby.

I don't even know his name. Yet I named my daughter after his mother! She wasn't usually so impulsive, but the past few months had forced her to be more flexible, more spontaneous. If she wasn't, she could die.

The nurse returned, wheeling a crib ahead of her. "Your little darling's just woken up and announced that she'd like her breakfast." She lifted Sarah from her crib, waiting for Beth to unfasten her gown.

"I'm Carol and I'll be looking after you," she said with a warm smile. "We'll run through the bathing routine later and you can ask me any questions about caring for your baby." She placed Sarah in her arms.

Overwhelming love filled Beth's heart and tears of joy filled her eyes as she gazed down at her daughter. Sarah started to fuss a little so Beth touched her cheek. When Sarah turned toward her breast and latched on, Beth winced at the sudden force of the baby's suction.

"Relax," the nurse urged. "I've got a few more moms to look in on. If you need any help in the meantime, use the call button beside your bed. You're welcome to get up and take a shower. Make yourself comfortable." She left, closing the door behind her.

Beth held on to the tiny hand that had worked its way out of the baby blanket. "You're so beautiful," she cooed and kissed her daughter's hand as Sarah suckled contentedly.

Beth wondered about the stranger. Would she ever see him again? Had he told his mom about the woman he'd rescued who'd named her daughter after her?

Beth's solitary existence since the sudden death of her husband had felt awkward at first. Now, after going through the grieving process, the sorrow and anger, the frustration and despair, she'd emerged a new woman. An independent woman who had to live by her wits.

She owed the stranger a debt of gratitude and should at the very least write him a note of thanks. The doctor seemed to know him. Perhaps she'd pass on the note?

On second thought, maybe that wasn't a good idea. Beth didn't want to get too friendly—with anyone.

Her heart constricted at the loneliness of her life. Compelled by circumstances to turn her back on friendships and family and rely on her own company, she longed to have someone she could confide in, someone who'd listen and not judge. Someone to be there at night when the demons called.

Don't think about it! There's no point in hanging on to the past. You're not alone anymore. Now you have Sarah, she told herself sternly and glanced down at her baby. So precious, so vulnerable. *Nothing bad will happen,* she promised her daughter. *We'll be fine. No one knows where we are. No one's found us in four months. We're safe!*

LUKE PUT THROUGH A CALL to his sister-in-law, Judge Becky O'Malley.

"Hey, Luke, what can I do for you?" she greeted him. "I hear Matt birthed a baby beside the highway last night."

"You've been talking to Hank."

"No, Jessica down at the courthouse told me."

Luke winced. Matt had a point. Hank's gossiping *was* getting out of hand. "I'm sorry to call you at work, Becky, but I need your help."

"Sounds intriguing. Tell me more."

"Matt needs a wife."

There was spluttering at the other end of the line, then Becky said, "I really wish you'd warn me when you're going to say something outrageous. I just choked on my coffee and now it's all over my keyboard. Hang on."

Luke could hear the rustling and tapping, then she came on the line again. "Just why does Matt need a wife? Of all of you, I think he's the most closed to romance."

"Matt's the rock of our family, but he's lonely and I detected something in his voice this morning."

"Like what?" Becky imitated a deep voice. "Luke. I'm lonely. I need a wife."

Luke laughed. "You've been married to Will too long. That's exactly what *he'd* say. I thought I'd get more sense out of you."

"Nope, got yourself the wrong gal. Will's sense of humor has rubbed off on me and I kinda like it."

"Yeah, I guess you did need to lighten up." Luke couldn't resist teasing his formerly uptight sister-in-law.

"Speak for yourself, Mr. Grumpy."

"Touché. Now, can we get serious and talk business?"

"About finding Matt a wife? Sure. What can I do?"

BETH WAS FINISHING breakfast when there was a light knock at her door. She dabbed her mouth with her napkin and checked to make sure she'd done up her nightgown properly before inviting her caller in.

The smile froze on her face as her visitor stepped into

her room. He held an enormous bunch of flowers, but that wasn't what had her heart rate speeding.

A police officer! Her heart pounded harder as prickles of fear crept up her spine and a thousand questions demanded answers. How had they found her? Had they traced her grandmother's car? Damn! Why hadn't she gotten the plates changed or sold it?

"Ma'am?"

The deep voice was familiar and the tone was gentle and unthreatening. But Beth knew better—cops weren't to be trusted.

The man removed his hat. Dark brown hair was revealed, along with his intense dark brown eyes. "I'm Matt O'Malley," he said. "I brought you in last night."

Beth squeezed her eyes shut as she fought for control of her racing heart. The kindhearted stranger was a *cop?* How ironic! She opened her eyes and glared at him, daring him to approach.

"You're a cop!"

"The county sheriff to be more precise."

"But…but you weren't wearing a uniform last night."

"I don't always wear one. Yesterday was one of those days."

Scattered memories of the previous night surfaced. The distant sound of a siren, driving snow, a car's headlights blinding her, excruciating pain and her fear of not making it to the hospital in time. Yelling. She'd yelled a lot. She blushed. This man—this *police* man—had witnessed the birth of her daughter.

"I remember a siren now. Was that you?"

"Yes."

He paused as if waiting for her to say something. Maybe it was just a coincidence that he was here. She sent up a silent prayer of thanks that she'd used her grandmother's car to drive to Colorado. Gran had said it would be safer, that way she wouldn't risk anyone running a check on her own car's plates. Hennessey would've posted an APB on her vehicle the day she fled California. Terror began to choke her at the thought of what Hennessey would do to her—what he'd do to her precious baby—if he ever found them.

"Ma'am? Is there a problem?"

Beth fought the urge to throw back the covers, grab her sleeping daughter and flee. She had to try to remain calm even though her nerves were stretched to the breaking point. If Matt O'Malley detected her nervousness, he'd get suspicious and make inquiries—if he hadn't done so already. He wouldn't have to search far to learn the truth.

She made herself smile and said, "No, Sheriff, of course not. It…was just such a shock to…" She shook her head. "I mean, I wasn't expecting any visitors."

He smiled and stepped toward the bed. "I stopped by to give you these," he said almost shyly and handed her the pink roses.

Taken aback by the gesture, Beth managed to say, "Thank you," covering her nervousness by breathing in their delicate perfume, then laying them in her lap, not wanting him to see how badly her hands trembled. "They're lovely," she said and wondered if this was just a social visit, after all. "You really didn't have to. You did more than enough for me last night."

"All in the line of duty." He placed his hat on the chair and looked into the crib where Sarah slept peacefully. "She's beautiful," he said softly, and Beth didn't miss the note of wonder in his voice.

He glanced up and cleared his throat. "I wanted to make sure you were both okay and to apologize for the way I lit out of here last night. I…I'm not good around, er, that is, I…"

"You don't have a stomach for…certain situations?"

He gave a self-deprecating grin. "How'd you guess?"

Regardless of her mistrust of cops, she couldn't help smiling at his obvious discomfort. His quick reactions the previous night had likely saved both their lives, hers and Sarah's. "I recall that when I told you the baby was coming, you moved very fast."

He dug his index finger between his collar and his throat and swallowed. Despite her fear, Beth found the gesture oddly endearing.

"I…owe you a huge debt of gratitude. I don't know what would've happened if you hadn't come along when you did. The road was so deserted, I don't know how long it would've been before another vehicle showed up." She paused, remembering. "Except for the other car I almost hit head-on… Was that you?"

"No. I was following you. And you owe your survival more to the safety features of your car than to anything I did."

Reaching into his top pocket, he withdrew his notebook. "I need to ask you a few questions if you don't mind."

PANIC FLITTED ACROSS her face for an instant before she got it under control. Her eyes narrowed and her chin rose defiantly. "You weren't driving a sheriff's department car," she challenged. "Surely you were off duty?"

"I drive an unmarked vehicle and, as county sheriff, I'm on call 24/7," he said. "Now, do you have your license?"

"Why do you need it?"

"So I can complete the details for my report."

"But…no one was injured. Why do you need to make a report?"

Matt's senses went on alert. She was acting strange. Sometimes friendly, sometimes fearful, sometimes combative. What was going on?

"Is there some reason you don't want me to see your license?"

"Of course not," she answered too quickly. "I didn't mean to question you. I guess in my haste to get to the hospital I left my license at home."

He made a mental note to check with Hank exactly what, in the way of possessions, they'd found in her car after towing it in.

"So you live around here?"

Again, he saw her gaze dart nervously around the room and wondered why she was so anxious.

He forced warmth into his smile, then said, "You mentioned that there wasn't anyone I should call, so I was curious as to why you were here in Peaks County in an advanced stage of pregnancy without anyone nearby you could turn to." He shrugged. "Seems strange to me, that's all."

"I...I only moved here recently—to Denver," she added, twisting the sheets in her fingers.

"Then why were you driving in the high country at midnight? In a blizzard?"

"I'd...been to dinner with a client in, ah, South Ridge and was heading home. I went into labor really fast."

She must think he was born yesterday with an excuse like that. "I take it your meeting went later than you planned? It's a long drive to Denver." He resisted the urge to say, *Without your license.*

At the sudden relief in her features, Matt knew she was making the story up as she went along and thought he'd given her an out.

"Yes...that's right."

She wasn't a convincing liar, probably because she hadn't had much experience. Her fists were so tightly clamped on the sheets. Her fear was almost palpable. But fear of what?

"I didn't know where the hospital was and...I got lost."

Yeah, right! No one would be caught out late in a near blizzard, then expect to make it back to Denver. Anyone in that situation would've stayed in South Ridge; it had some decent motels. And no one would be foolish enough to drive around looking for a hospital while in such intense pain. Surely Beth Ford had a cell phone.... She didn't look dumb. She looked bone-deep scared. More than ever, he was convinced she was lying through her teeth.

"You referred to clients. What do you do?"

"Why do you want to know?"

He shrugged again in an effort to appear unthreatening. "Just making conversation. I wondered what might keep you out so late in weather like last night's."

"You make it sound as though I'm up to something sinister."

Matt held up his hands. "No, not at all. I was just curious."

She finally stopped twisting the sheets into a knot and fixed him with a steady gaze. "I'm an architect."

Matt's eyebrows rose a little at that. She'd stopped worrying the sheets, so maybe that at least was the truth. "You've been too busy with moving and the baby coming to get around to changing your license plates?" he suggested.

Her expression eased further and he watched her smooth the sheets, pressing out the creases with shaky fingers.

"Yes, that's right." Her look was one of innocent inquiry as she asked, "Was there anything wrong in not attending to it sooner?"

He couldn't help admiring her for neatly turning the situation around by questioning him about changing her plates. "State law requires that if you're living and working in Colorado, you have thirty days to change them," he said, then immediately wanted to swallow his words. This woman didn't need Colorado law shoved down her throat. More than anything, she needed compassion.

She was lying because she was scared, and something about her stirred a desire within him to protect her and her baby.

The heat burned in his gut. This was foolishness. So he'd rescued a woman in labor. It didn't make up for Sally and the baby. Nothing could ever absolve him of the guilt of letting them die alone. He concentrated on the present situation instead and glanced at the baby in her crib. His heart melted.

She was yawning, her tiny mouth forming a perfect O. She sure looked a whole lot prettier than she had last night. Her formerly screwed-up red face was a soft pink and fair down covered her head.

As though aware of his scrutiny Sarah began to squirm a little, then she started to cry. Matt reached out to quiet her, his big hand brushing her arm in a comforting gesture. She grasped his finger.

The kid had a fierce grip! *Like mother, like daughter,* he thought, but there was something nice about someone wanting to hold you so tight.

Beth leaned over to get her baby from the crib.

"It's okay. I've got her," he said and picked her up, careful to wrap Sarah in the blanket that had fallen away. He held her protectively against him and cooed to her.

BETH WAS TERRIFIED. On the one hand, she didn't want this *police*man near her daughter. On the other, he seemed to know what he was doing, which was more than she could say for herself. She hadn't been able to rewrap Sarah properly into the tight bundle she'd been before she'd unwound the blanket to count all her fingers and toes and to kiss her tiny hands and feet.

"What have you done to yourself, missy?" he asked when Sarah continued to fuss. He placed her on the bed. "Got yourself all undone. Don't you know babies are supposed to stay wrapped up so they feel safe and protected?"

Beth watched, fascinated, as he expertly rewrapped her daughter into a semblance of the little bundle she'd been before her investigations.

"You…you obviously know what you're doing," she said, trying to keep the envy from her voice.

"Sorry. I didn't mean to take over." His hands touched hers as he put the baby in her arms.

She cradled Sarah against her and asked, "Have you got children of your own?"

THE HOT, BURNING KNIFE of guilt twisted inside him. Damn! Why had he allowed himself to be drawn into this? He took a deep breath. He wasn't going to lose it now. It'd been three years. He needed to move on. That was what everyone said.

Yet the pain bit deeper. Three long, lonely years. He had to get on with his life and stop feeling sick with guilt every time someone asked him if he had kids.

"Sheriff? Are you all right?"

Matt pulled himself together and said, "I've got four nieces and an adopted nephew."

Sarah settled for a moment and then started to fuss again, her tiny arms struggling to get out of the blanket. Beth's brows drew together. "Surely she can't be hungry again?"

Sarah let out a cry.

"What's wrong?" she pleaded.

When the baby started to scream, Matt mused that she had her mother's lungs. "What goes in must come out."

She looked up at him. "Oh. Of course."

The door swung open and a nurse breezed into the room and stood over her. "What are you doing to my little darlin'?" she admonished lightly as she lifted Sarah from her mother's arms. "I think you need a change, sweet Sarah. Let's leave your mama here with Sheriff O'Malley and come back when we're nice to be near again, huh?"

"You've got yourself a gem," Matt observed as she left the room. He scooped up his hat from the chair. He hadn't felt so unsettled in the presence of a woman in a long time and needed to get out of there. Beth was too wound up at the moment to answer any further questions, so he wouldn't press her. He'd find out the truth soon enough.

BETH WATCHED MATT worrying the brim of his hat and almost regretted he was leaving. He was so caring and capable with Sarah. But he *was* a cop and he was asking her questions she didn't want to answer. The sooner she put distance between them, the better.

"I'll stop by and see you both again tomorrow," he said.

"No!" she cried, then caught herself, not wanting to seem too eager to be rid of him. "I mean, you've done more than enough for us.... It's really not necessary, Sheriff O'Malley."

"It's Matt, and it isn't any trouble. I'd like to see how my mom's namesake is doing."

Beth couldn't very well refuse to let him visit. It would only serve to make him more suspicious and she sure didn't want that. Forcing a warm smile, she said with as much enthusiasm as she could, "All right. That would be nice."

After Matt had tipped the brim of his hat in a tiny salute and left, Beth stared at the closed door and released her breath. That had been a close call! She didn't want him tracing her back to L.A. and asking questions. Somehow she had to get word to her mother and Gran that she and the baby were fine.

For four long months she'd endured an enforced silence, not able to phone them, write or e-mail in case Hennessey traced her through them. Although it had been Gran's idea to lend Beth her car, if Matt O'Malley did a trace on her number plates, they'd lead him straight to her grandmother. And the police computers back in L.A. would show that a cop in Colorado had run a check on them.

She closed her eyes and tried to dispel the fear rising within her at the thought of Detective John Hennessey threatening her grandmother, the way he'd threatened her.

MATT LEANED BACK at his desk and rubbed his eyes. The events of the night before were taking their toll.

He called Hank to find out what personal items Beth had left behind in her vehicle, but Hank informed him he'd already had her purse and suitcase delivered to her at the hospital.

Matt cursed softly. For once, the man was being efficient, although he wasn't sure Hank hadn't sneaked a peek inside that purse of hers. "Okay, thanks. And, Hank? Could you arrange to get some estimates for fixing her car?" Hank knew every repair shop in the county and would see that she got an honest price.

"Sure," he agreed readily. "It's the least we can do for the little lady. I guess the last thing she'd wanna be bothered with when she gets outta the hospital would be runnin' around gettin' quotes on fixin' her car." He paused for a moment. "Say, Matt—"

"Hank," Matt interrupted, not wanting to get caught up in a long-winded discussion with the county gossip. "Something's come up and I gotta go," he said and hung up. He leaned back in his chair again, stretched his arms above his head and thought about Beth Ford.

Hank's mention of a suitcase raised his suspicion that she hadn't come from Denver to visit a client. Denver was less than a two hours' drive back down the interstate. Since the interstate was often closed during heavy storms because of the avalanche danger, it would've made sense for her to stay somewhere until the blizzard let up. More than ever, Matt believed she'd been on her way to the hospital from somewhere in the county.

He glanced out the window. The snow had started falling in big fat flakes, obliterating his view of the mountains surrounding Spruce Lake. He loved his hometown and had no desire to ever live anywhere else. Even after Sally and the baby died, he couldn't bear the thought of leaving, of making a fresh start somewhere else. The mountains were part of him and of his close-knit family. The ranch he grew up on, plus his family and friends, were all he needed in the world. At least, that was what Matt tried to tell himself whenever the loneliness and the pain of loss seemed about to consume him.

He pushed the memories aside and turned his mind to Beth's strange behavior. He was glad it had occurred to him to ask Hank for estimates. She'd have enough problems with an infant to care for and no husband or friends nearby to help.

That intrigued him. Why *didn't* she have anyone close by? If she'd been telling the truth about living in Denver, it wasn't a long trip for someone to pay her a visit in the hospital, yet she'd seemed surprised to get even one visitor. Maybe she hadn't made any friends here yet. That begged yet another question. Why would a widow in the advanced stages of pregnancy move away from her family and friends?

Beth Ford was an enigma.

But Matt was determined she wouldn't stay one for long.

Chapter Three

While Sarah slept, Beth took a lengthy shower, then ate lunch. Soon afterward, Dr. Lucy Cochrane dropped by to see her.

"I don't usually do night shifts but I was filling in for a friend last night when Matt brought you in," she explained as she examined Beth and then Sarah.

"You're both doing well," she announced a few minutes later. "And you don't seem to have suffered any ill effects from the car accident, either," she said, winding up her stethoscope and slipping it in the pocket of her white jacket. "You can probably check out tomorrow. Although I prefer first-time mothers to stay a little longer."

Beth nodded vaguely. She'd already decided to check out of the hospital before then—today if possible. She didn't want any more visits from the sheriff and needed to get back to the safety of her cabin in the mountains.

Lucy perched on the side of the bed. "Now, is there anything else you need? Any information or advice?"

Beth was tempted to bring up Matt O'Malley and then immediately wondered why. Okay, so the guy had been kind enough to Sarah, but he asked her questions she didn't want to answer. Questions that could reveal a lot more than she wanted him or anyone else to know.

Although Lucy spoke fondly of Matt, she hadn't offered

any personal information about him other than to assure Beth she'd been in safe hands in spite of Matt's weak stomach.

Lucy glanced at her watch and said, "I'd better hit the road. I've got to pick up my youngest from day care."

After suggesting she take Sarah to the nursery so Beth could catch up on her sleep, Lucy said goodbye and left, pushing the crib ahead of her.

Bone-weary, Beth snuggled beneath the covers and took a nap.

SHE WAS AWAKENED by Carol, the nurse, returning with Sarah from the nursery, her baby's lungs at full throttle.

Still unsure what to do for her newborn, how to figure out every nuance of every sound she made, Beth prayed she'd soon learn and breathed a sigh of relief when Sarah latched on to her food supply.

The trouble was, she hadn't been around babies much. The only child of only children, she had no cousins, aunts or uncles. Although some of her girlfriends back in L.A. had children, apart from admiring them at a distance, Beth hadn't contemplated motherhood. Until she'd found herself pregnant.

Stunned was the only way to describe her reaction. Marcus was less than pleased. Starting a family had been put onto the back burner for later on, when they were more financially secure. But that had all come to an end the day Marcus was killed. Killed by a fellow cop.

SARAH HAD JUST FINISHED feeding when there was a knock at the door. Beth froze, fearing it was the sheriff returning.

A woman with a mass of red curls popped her head

around the door. "Hi," she said. Then, uninvited, she advanced into the room.

She was impeccably well-groomed in a smart dress suit and smiled a little too brightly, reminding Beth of people who sold religion door-to-door.

"I'm Becky O'Malley."

Beth didn't want to meet any more of Sheriff Matt O'Malley's family. They might press her for information on his behalf. "I wasn't expecting visitors," she said, her tone chilly, hoping the other woman would take the hint and depart.

Undaunted, the woman grinned and said, "I'm married to Matt's brother Will."

"May I ask why you're here?"

She smiled, apparently not in the least put off by Beth's attitude. "Luke thought I should come and visit you. He said you didn't know anyone in town and as this baby's practically an O'Malley—" she leaned forward and stroked Sarah's cheek "—we couldn't have you not getting any visitors or thinking we're unfriendly, could we?"

Beth held her daughter closer. "*Who* is Luke?"

"Matt's oldest brother. He runs the family ranch." She returned her attention to Sarah.

Beth cleared her throat.

Becky looked up and, as if finally noticing her discomfort, said, "I'm sorry. I've barged my way in here, assuming you'd welcome a visitor, and I didn't realize maybe that isn't what you want."

Although Beth fought to keep her guard up, there was something sincere about the woman, a genuine warmth. Now she looked hurt.

"I'll leave you in peace," she said and got to her feet.

"No…" Beth laid a restraining hand on her arm. "I'm the one who should be sorry. I'm just a little…tired and overwhelmed." She shrugged. "I wasn't expecting visitors."

Becky grinned. "May I?" she asked, indicating Sarah.

Beth didn't see any harm in allowing the other woman to hold Sarah and, wanting to make amends for her earlier rudeness, passed the baby to her. "Sheriff O'Malley said he has four nieces and a nephew. Um, no kids of his own?"

Becky shook her head. "He…used to be married" She looked up from stroking Sarah's cheek and smiled. "I have a son, Nicolas, and a six-month-old, Lily. She's with her daddy today," she explained. "My brother-in-law, Luke, who's divorced, has three adorable daughters. The other two brothers, Jack and Adam, aren't married. Yet." She raised her eyebrows to indicate that if she had any say in it, they wouldn't be bachelors for much longer. "Jack's a contractor and lives in town. Adam's the youngest of the boys. He's a firefighter and recently moved to Boulder." She resumed her cooing to Sarah. "She's gorgeous. You should be very proud."

Beth felt a sense of motherly pride at the candid compliment. It didn't matter that this woman was related to a cop, Beth decided; she liked her. "Thank you."

Becky used her free hand to dig into her carryall and produce a beautifully wrapped box.

"I thought you might like some chocolate," she said.

Taken aback by the other woman's generosity, Beth could barely stutter out her thanks. Why were these strangers being so nice to her? She unwrapped the gift, then offered the box to Becky who selected a chocolate and bit into it. "Mmm, yum," she said around the sticky confection. "It would almost be worth getting pregnant again so I can eat a whole box by myself!"

The woman was irrepressible. For the first time in

months, Beth laughed. Oh, how she'd missed the companionship of other women.

Becky beamed and stuck out her hand. "Friends?"

Beth shook it. "Friends."

"I like you," Becky said in a frank voice and took another chocolate. "Is it true Matt got you here with moments to spare?"

Beth nodded and then flushed at the memory of how she'd demanded he stay with her.

"And he really hung around for Sarah's birth?"

Beth was starting to feel uncomfortable again. "Matt told you?"

"Heavens, no! Matt's the poster boy for discretion. I heard it on the town grapevine."

Beth swallowed. This was the problem with hiding out in a small town. News traveled fast. Maybe her cabin wasn't so safe anymore.

"Ye-es. Matt stayed with me for Sarah's birth," she said, hoping that would appease Becky.

"Just wait till his mother hears about that!" Becky exclaimed.

"I guess she'll hear sometime, since I named Sarah after her."

Becky's eyes opened wide. "Really?"

"I couldn't very well call her, Matt," she pointed out.

Becky laughed. "No, indeed!" She addressed Sarah. "We can't have such a beautiful little pumpkin named after ugly old Matt, can we, sweetie?"

An image of Matt standing tentatively at her door this morning came to Beth. She'd never describe him as ugly. Ruggedly handsome was far more appropriate.

Now, where did that come from? she wondered as a warm flush suffused her body.

"Beth?"

She raised her head to find Becky looking at her quizzically.

"You were a million miles away."

"I...I guess I'm just tired."

"And that's my cue to leave." After placing a kiss on Sarah's cheek, she handed her back. "Get as much sleep as you can while you're here," she advised. "Believe me, you won't get any once you get her home. If I can, I'd like to visit you tomorrow, if that's all right."

Beth couldn't very well refuse. "Thanks. I look forward to it."

Becky grinned that infectious grin of hers. "Great. In the meantime, if you need anything, please feel free to give me a call." She passed her a business card.

Beth accepted it. "Thank you. You've been very kind," she said, almost regretting she wouldn't be here tomorrow when Becky came by. She was going to leave the hospital and head back to her cabin in the mountains long before Matt O'Malley or any of his relatives turned up again. As for her grandmother's car, it was now a liability. She almost wished it had been damaged enough to end up in a wrecker's yard somewhere.

MATT WAS DEALING with a mountain of paperwork when Becky phoned later that afternoon to say she'd been to visit Beth, that she liked her and thought Sarah was adorable. "How did you find out?" he growled, knowing full well that Lucy wouldn't have said anything about her patient, even to Becky.

"Luke called to suggest I go and make Beth feel welcome, since your folks are off sailing around the Caribbean. He said she's from California, so he thought she might not have any friends nearby."

"And she won't be staying around much longer if any of you interfere, so butt out."

"Be fair, Matt. She's alone in the middle of Colorado with a new baby. How would *you* feel in her situation?"

"I don't know. I've never had a baby," he noted drily.

"Aren't you the tiniest bit curious about why she's here?"

Matt was very curious, but he wasn't about to admit it. "I'm sure she has her reasons. The point is, she and her baby are safe and well, and I don't see what business it is of yours to go visiting her."

"For goodness' sake, Matt!"

Matt could hear her indignant huff on the other end of the line and smiled.

"Her baby is practically an O'Malley," Becky said primly. "Beth said she named Sarah after your mom."

"And I think that's where the family connection should end, don't you?" Matt couldn't keep the impatience from his voice. His family was altogether too nosy.

"I liked her," Becky said again. Her voice held a trace of hurt. "She's all alone. I was only trying to help."

Matt rubbed a weary hand over his face. "I'm sorry, Becky, but I'm not sure I trust her," he admitted, "and I think you're better off staying away from her."

"What's not to trust?"

"Just about everything." He leaned back, pushed the papers on his desk aside and lifted his legs onto it. Maybe it was worth discussing this with Becky. She'd given sage advice in the past. "Her name. What she's doing here alone without any support. Her marital status."

"You think she's hiding something?"

"Uh-huh." Matt scratched his head.

"My take?" Becky said. "She's either a widow, as she says, or recently separated or divorced."

"How can you tell?"

"Her wedding band. Or rather, the mark it's left. Her ring finger is paler where the band should be. When you've worn a ring for several years, it takes a long time for the tan mark to disappear. Hers is still faintly visible."

Matt sat forward in his chair. "Are you positive?"

"Absolutely. She was definitely wearing some kind of ring up until the past few months."

MATT FINISHED HIS WORK for the day and contemplated another hospital visit. Becky's remark about Sarah being practically an O'Malley had been playing through his mind all day.

He did feel a connection to Sarah, no doubt because of his role in her birth. She was so vulnerable. He couldn't help wondering why her mother needed to tell so many lies. That made him wonder, too, about Sarah's safety if Beth was in trouble. She'd sure looked scared when he'd pressed her for information.

He glanced at his watch and swore. By the time he got to the hospital, it'd be after nine. Visiting hours were over at eight-thirty. He shrugged into his jacket before stepping outside into the softly falling snow.

Plenty of time tomorrow, he decided. Meantime, he was going to drop in on Luke and set him straight on a few things.

"WHAT'S SHE LOOK like?" Luke inquired.

Matt had only just arrived at the ranch; he'd immediately told Luke to stop siccing Becky on to Beth.

"Didn't Becky tell you?" he asked sarcastically.

"She was too busy telling me about Sarah and how cute she is to fit in a description of her mom."

Matt considered how he'd describe Beth. Seeing her

felt like…coming *home*. Somewhere he never wanted to leave. She had a quiet, inner beauty, an innocence and vulnerability, he found appealing, in spite of her amateur attempts at lying.

He sighed. Who was he kidding? The woman disliked him and everything he represented. Why did he care what his family thought or did about her?

Because she's scared and alone, a small voice said.

Matt raked his hand through his hair. "She's probably in her late twenties. She's got longish blond hair and gray eyes."

"Sounds kinda vague."

"We haven't spent that much time together," Matt snapped, in no mood for idle chitchat. "She didn't have her license, so I couldn't confirm the details."

"Is she tall? Short? Cuddly? Skinny?"

"She's just had a baby!" Matt exploded, fed up with his brother's prying.

Unmoved by his reaction, Luke crossed his arms and waited.

Matt sighed again, resigned. His brother wasn't going to give up till he'd gotten what he wanted. Having a conversation with Luke was usually like pulling teeth from a hen, so he guessed he'd better make the most of it. "She's the stereotypical California girl. Faint freckles across her nose… Nice lips."

Matt didn't like Luke's lazy smile. "What're you grinning about?"

"You. You've got a dreamy look in your eyes."

"I didn't pay that much attention to her." But that was a lie and Matt knew it.

"You noticed her eye color and that she has freckles and nice lips," Luke pointed out.

"I'm a cop. I'm trained to notice stuff like that," Matt

grumbled and climbed back into his vehicle. The only way he was going to avoid answering any more of Luke's questions was to get out of there. "Good night, Luke," he said and turned the ignition key. "Stay away from Beth Ford. She's none of your business!" he warned and peeled away from the ranch.

Chapter Four

Jealousy. It was jealousy, pure and simple, Matt decided the next morning. Jealousy had twisted his guts and had him up pacing the floor half the night.

No sooner had he gotten home than his backstabbing brother had called and practically intimated that Beth would make a perfect wife for *him* and a mother to his three daughters!

The lousy rat hadn't even met her, yet he was already planning a future for Beth and Sarah. What the hell was Luke playing at?

Matt downed a cup of coffee and headed for the bathroom to get ready. He was going to make damn sure Luke didn't beat him to the hospital before visiting hours commenced.

WHEN HE STRODE THROUGH the hospital doors an hour later, Matt was trying to assure himself for the umpteenth time that he wasn't visiting Beth for any selfish reasons related to his own need for a woman's company or because she interested him. No, he was only there so early to make sure Luke didn't have a chance to put crazy notions of happily-ever-after-on-the-ranch into Beth's head when she was feeling so vulnerable.

He wasn't interested in her for himself, merely felt some

sort of responsibility for her and Sarah. He wanted to protect her from—

Matt halted in the corridor outside her room. *Protect? Responsibility?* He'd sworn off getting involved with anyone, loving anyone, after Sally and the baby died. He never wanted to expose himself to that sort of pain again.

So why, then, were they continually invading his thoughts?

He could hear a baby's loud cry from Beth's room. He knocked, but when there was no answer, other than the rising pitch of Sarah's cries, he turned the knob and opened the door.

Beth was rocking Sarah, her head bent over her daughter as she spoke softly, trying to calm her baby.

Despite the lies she might have told him, Matt couldn't deny that her love and concern for the child were genuine.

He coughed politely and Beth looked up. Her eyes were sunken with fatigue, her hair was unbrushed and her nightgown pulled carelessly together. But to Matt she was beautiful.

"I didn't hear you come in." She sniffed and reached for a tissue. "How long have you been there?"

Sarah continued to fuss, her plaintive cries of distress filling the room. Matt's heart went out to both of them.

"Long enough to know you've probably had it. May I?" he asked and, at Beth's nod, scooped Sarah from her mother's arms and held her against him.

The baby sensed the change at once and quieted.

"Typical!" Beth fumed. "There doesn't seem to be anything I can do for her. I've hardly slept a wink all night."

Matt stroked Sarah's cheek, then looked back at Beth. She was trying so hard to do the right thing by her daughter. "Do you want to take a minute to wash your face? I'm happy to hold her."

Beth scrambled out of bed. "Thanks. I must really look a mess." She went into her bathroom, but didn't close the door.

Matt could hear the sound of running water, then it shut off. "Becky came to visit yesterday," she called out.

Matt didn't miss the note of longing in her voice. "She wasn't too pushy, was she? My family tends to specialize in taking over. Particularly the women." And Luke.

"She was very sweet," Beth told him, returning to her room. "She seems to have great affection for you."

Matt grinned. "We're a very close family." He used the opening to question her. "Do you have any family?"

Her expression changed, but Matt pressed her. She was being far too mysterious. Maybe she was a battered woman claiming to be widowed to try and stop him from delving deeper. If so, he was determined to find out and protect her. "Are your parents still alive? Your husband's folks?"

Beth shook her head. "I'm an only child. That's why I know almost nothing about looking after babies," she said, neatly ducking his question. "My career was my life and I steered clear of getting too involved with children. Until I got pregnant, I didn't think I could love and raise a child of my own."

"And now?"

She smiled and her shoulders relaxed a little. "Now I know I'm capable of loving a child. Although I'm not sure I would've admitted that at around two this morning when she was screaming at the top of her lungs." She stroked Sarah's hair and looked up at him, the devotion she felt for her daughter evident in her eyes.

Matt liked it when she was being frank with him. It made him feel trusted.

"Can I ask why you're here again?"

Matt was caught off guard by her question and said the first thing that came into his head. "I meant to tell you yesterday that your car's been towed to a garage and I've arranged to have some estimates done."

He saw her swallow before she said, "Thank you, but I intended to take care of all that when I get out of here."

"It's no problem. In the meantime, it's safe. I wanted you to know that."

Feeling awkward at the silence that filled the room, he addressed Sarah. "Have you inherited your mama's lungs, sweetie?"

"What do you mean?"

Matt glanced up from the baby lying contentedly in his arms. "Ah, the other night, you were making enough noise to wake the dead."

Her face flushed with embarrassment. "I'm sorry. I was scared...and in so much pain."

Matt smiled. "No need to apologize. The experience affirmed my everlasting gratitude that men can't give birth." He shifted Sarah to his shoulder when she started to fuss again and rubbed her back.

"You're so good with her," she said, her voice full of longing.

"When my nieces were babies, I could calm them when everyone else was at the breaking point." The admission had him wondering for the thousandth time what sort of father he would've made.

Beth's shoulders relaxed some more. "That's nice. You'll make a great father someday."

He wished she wouldn't keep talking about fatherhood.

"I'll bet you're the one the kids turn to when they need advice or want to keep a secret from their parents?"

Matt forced the burning sensation aside and nodded. "You guessed it."

Sarah rewarded his back rubbing with an enormous burp. Then she threw up.

Matt held his breath as he felt the warm liquid seep through his shirt. He handed Sarah back to her mother and left the room without a word.

TOO AWARE OF HIS absence, Beth wondered if he'd come back. Although she'd planned to be long gone by the time Matt O'Malley showed up this morning, things hadn't gone to plan. Sarah had kept her up most of the night alternately crying and feeding. Now here she was, feeling like death warmed over and still at the hospital. She was in no state to make her way home and try to manage Sarah while she was so exhausted. It wouldn't hurt to stay another day, so long as Matt didn't push her for any more answers to his questions.

Beth looked down at her daughter and couldn't believe her eyes. She'd fallen asleep. "Typical!" she muttered again. "Keep me up all night and *now* you want to sleep!"

After cleaning Sarah's face and hands, she placed her in the crib.

Despite not wanting to see Matt today, she was grateful he'd shown up, if only to give her a break from Sarah.

When she'd seen him standing there, looking so dependable, his eyes full of compassion, Beth had felt gratitude right down to her toes.

Careful! she warned herself. *It isn't wise to rely on Matt O'Malley. He's a cop.*

In her mind she believed this, but her heart was having trouble agreeing. Ever since he'd lifted her from the car, she'd felt safe, protected. The way he'd held her securely against him as he carried her to his vehicle had penetrated through the pain, instilling a sense of calm and sheltering her from her fear of what was to come. And he hadn't deserted her when he'd got her to the hospital. Instead, he'd stayed, held her hand and provided her with some focus outside the pain of childbirth.

No matter how hard she tried to deny it, she felt a bond with Matt O'Malley.

When a light knock sounded at the door, Beth glanced up, hoping Matt had returned.

The man who stood in the doorway bore every indication of being a close relative of Matt's. He was tall, with thick, dark brown hair graying at the temples, brown eyes and a lazy smile. He held a large bunch of flowers. "Hi, there. I'm Luke O'Malley," he said. "May I come in?"

Since it would be downright rude to refuse, she said, "Of course. Matt's just stepped out for a moment."

Luke advanced toward her bed. "I brought you these to cheer up your room," he said and laid the flowers in her arms. "Becky told me she visited you yesterday, so I knew you'd only get candy from her."

"You seem to know your sister-in-law very well." She smiled and offered her hand. "I'm Beth, and thank you. The flowers are lovely."

He shook her hand, and Beth noted that she didn't experience the same wonderful feeling as when Matt had accidentally touched her the day before.

"Pleased to meet you," he drawled and released her hand. "Matt's told me a lot about you, and I'm pleased to make your acquaintance at last."

He turned his attention to Sarah lying peacefully asleep in her crib. "Now, isn't she just the prettiest little lady? Reminds me of my own beautiful daughters when they were babies. You'll have to come out to the ranch and meet them. They've grown up into beautiful girls. 'Course they miss having a mom—"

"Luke!" Matt stood in the doorway; his expression was thunderous.

Deep in her belly, Beth felt a prickle of something she couldn't quite name. Sarah stirred in her crib.

"Hush, Matt! Now look what you've done," Luke admonished. "You've gone and woken the little darlin' up."

IMMEDIATELY SUSPICIOUS of the stupid grin his brother wore, Matt narrowed his eyes in warning. He'd watched Luke weave his charm from the doorway and didn't like it one bit.

He moved to Sarah's crib and lifted her into his arms. "There, there, sweetie," he soothed, and Sarah rewarded him by returning immediately to sleep.

Luke had resumed his pathetic attempts to charm Beth, oozing his best country-bumpkin charm and prattling on about her and Sarah coming to visit *his* ranch. Last time Matt had heard, Two Elk belonged to *all* the O'Malleys!

Luke was saying, "Just give me a call and I'll come and get you."

Fixing his brother with a look of contempt, Matt snarled, "Hadn't you better be getting along? I'm sure you've got calves to brand or torture in some other diabolical way."

When Luke refused to budge, Matt suspected he was up to something, and if his instincts were right, Becky was in collusion with him.

Luke crossed his arms over his chest and set his feet at a wider stance. "Now, now, Matt, you can't go keeping Beth all to yourself. I'm sure she'd like to meet the rest of the *single* O'Malley men."

Luke's challenging stance meant he thought he was settling in for a long session. Matt needed to get him out of there, and fast.

"Like I was saying, haven't you got a whole barn full of animals waiting back at the ranch for you to torment?" Matt said, holding Sarah protectively against him.

A slow grin spread across his brother's face. "That I do," he agreed, a little too readily, making Matt even more suspicious about his motives.

His stomach sank to his boots when Luke said, "Seems my little brother's in an awful hurry to be left alone with you, so I'll be taking my leave, if you don't mind." He turned and winked at Matt, then slipped out the door.

Matt stole a glance at Beth. Her face was bright red with embarrassment. He didn't know what to say in answer to Luke's parting shot. He'd been set up and he hadn't seen it coming! The silence in the room stretched to a minute, then two. He wished Sarah would start fussing, but she slept on, contented in his arms.

BETH FIDGETED WITH the sheet. Was Luke implying that Matt was…*interested* in her? Surely not! They hardly knew each other.

She changed the subject. "Becky said you're a widower."

From his pained look, she knew she'd struck a raw nerve.

He put Sarah in her crib, tenderly covered her with the blanket, then raised his head. "My wife died three years ago," he murmured.

The agony she saw etched in his eyes made her regret her prying. "And you're still in love with her," she said softly.

"*No.*" He spoke too quickly and drew his hand through

his hair in what seemed to be an uncharacteristically nervous gesture.

He stood and said, "I'd…better be off. But first I want to apologize for that outburst earlier. I think my busybody of a brother was trying to matchmake. It was inappropriate and I'm sorry for any embarrassment it caused you."

Matt O'Malley was blushing! Beth found it touching.

"It didn't embarrass me," she told him, although that wasn't true. "And…I'm so sorry about your wife."

Matt gave her a curt nod and left.

"Phew!" Beth fanned her face after the door closed behind him. Questioning Matt about his wife sure had him heading out in a hurry. *He must still love her,* she thought, smoothing the sheets. *In spite of his denial.*

She nestled beneath the covers and thought about the sheriff. He was a complex man, an intriguing man. Big but gentle, physically strong yet weak stomached. She smiled at that one. He'd been so good-natured about Lucy's teasing in the delivery room. And he obviously cared about his family, just as they cared about him.

He had the one thing she'd always wanted—a big, loving family. She'd always craved siblings to play with, fight with and go on holidays with. Instead, she'd been a lonely child who'd had to rely on her own company. She supposed there was one benefit to her upbringing; it had stood her in good stead for the past months of enforced solitude.

There was something inherently appealing about a man who could grieve for his wife for years. *Unlike me,* she thought with a pang of conscience. She'd grieved more for the sham that was her marriage than for Marcus, after his treachery was revealed.

How could she have lived with someone for so long and not really known him?

THE DAY BEFORE Marcus's funeral, she'd found a safety-deposit-box key taped beneath a kitchen drawer.

While searching for a silver cake knife her mother-in-law had given them and now wanted back, she'd become frustrated when the drawer had stuck. Worn out with grief and exhaustion, she'd wrenched it so hard, it came completely off its runners. As she was trying to replace it, her fingers had made contact with something taped under it. She pulled off the tape and withdrew a key. It looked like the one Marcus claimed he'd returned to the bank after they'd installed a home safe.

Curious to see if it *was* the same key, she'd gone to the bank and used it. Turned out it fit their old safety-deposit box and inside were stacks of hundred-dollar bills and a notebook containing names and numbers. And another key.

Sickened, confused, she'd slammed the box shut and been about to stagger out of the vault. The bank security officer had seen her distress, suggested she rest for a moment and gotten her a glass of water. While she drank it, a dozen reasons why their former safety-deposit box would be full of money swam through her head. None of them made any sense—except the one that kept nagging her. *Marcus was a dirty cop.*

The second key had opened another box in the vault. However, this one was stuffed to the brim with bags of white powder. Stunned at the implications, she'd left the bank and gone through the motions at Marcus's police funeral, been given due respect by his fellow officers, sat by his grave, listened to the mournful wail of the bagpipes, accepted the folded flag.

And all this time she was wondering what to do. Just after midnight, Marcus's former partner, Detective John Hennessey, who'd made such a display of his grief during the funeral service, had come to the house, demanding the key.

Terrified, Beth knew that if she handed it over, her life would end as surely as Marcus's had. So she'd played dumb, deflecting the issue by admitting they had a safe. Did he mean the key to that? Hennessey had dragged her by her hair to the safe and told her to open it. Inside, all he'd found was her jewelry and some stock certificates.

Infuriated, he'd commanded his henchman, "Morgan! Search the place. Tear it apart."

Morgan ransacked the house, dumping the contents of drawers on the floor, tearing down curtains and slicing through her leather sofas and the canvases covering her walls in his frenzied hunt for the key.

As Morgan wreaked devastation on her once-lovely home, one certainty kept emerging—these men couldn't afford to leave any loose ends lying around. If she gave Hennessey the key, he'd kill her to cover their tracks. If she didn't hand it over, he'd still kill her. She needed to buy time to figure out what to do.

When Morgan returned from the master bedroom, shaking his head, Hennessey snatched the knife from his hand and held the blade against her belly.

"I'll give you twenty-four hours," he whispered, menace dripping from every word. "Or else."

"Or else what?" she asked, pretending not to understand, hoping to convince him she was as ignorant of the whereabouts of that key as she'd been forty-eight hours earlier.

"Meaning," he growled, "that if you haven't called me by then, I'll come after you—" he turned the blade over so she could feel the point pressing against her abdomen "—and your baby."

Her intake of breath as she felt her baby move had him

sneering with triumph. "Twenty-four hours. You report this to *anyone,* you and your baby are dead. Understand?"

Mute with terror, Beth had nodded.

She'd sat amid the wreckage, weeping. Weeping for her dead husband and her sham of a marriage but mostly trembling with fear for her unborn child. By the time her tears were spent, any love she'd felt for Marcus Jackson had shriveled into a tiny, hard kernel of resentment and anger.

She couldn't go to the police. Hennessey *was* the police. How far could she trust Internal Affairs or the media? If she hadn't been pregnant, she would've considered IA or the newspapers, but her first concern was the safety of her baby. It was too risky to expose herself that way—at least until after her baby was born.

Beth called the only person she knew she could trust implicitly—her grandmother, Elizabeth Wyatt.

Her father's mom had been more mother than grand-mother to Beth. Her own mother, Patrice Whitman, was an actress who, after several minor Hollywood roles, had married James Wyatt, a respected L.A. stockbroker. Beth was conceived on their around-the-world honeymoon, and as Patrice liked to tell anyone within hearing distance, her daughter's birth was so painful and traumatic she swore she'd never go through it again. And she hadn't.

Patrice was at best a distant mother, devoted to James and throwing lavish parties. Since James's death in a boat-ing accident ten years previously, she'd traveled the world seeking "enlightenment." From ashrams in India to sweat lodges in Arizona. Patrice had exhausted just about every self-help, mind-expanding, navel-gazing ritual possible. She'd recently changed her name to Aurora and was cur-rently seeking messages in the northern lights north of the Arctic Circle.

By contrast, Beth's grandmother—after whom she'd been named—had been her rock throughout her life, her wise mentor, her best friend.

After telling Elizabeth what had happened—Hennessey's shocking revelations about Marcus and the evidence she had to support it—Beth told her grandmother that in order to protect her baby's life, she had to go into hiding until her child was born. And maybe after. She could have no further contact with anyone from her former life.

Always practical, her grandmother had agreed, then said, "I'll help you any way I can. What do you want me to do?"

Beth outlined her plans. She would leave L.A., disappear. Tomorrow she'd take some of the money from the safety-deposit box and live on it until the baby was born. When she was stronger and could leave the baby somewhere safe, she'd reveal everything about Hennessey. And repay the money, although she didn't know to whom. "I can't tell you where I'm going, because I'm not sure and I don't want to put you in any danger. And please, whatever you do, don't tell Mother about this. You know what a drama queen she is."

Elizabeth had snorted and said, "Actually, that might work well for you because when she files a missing person's report and they see the damage to your home, she'll kick up a hell of a stink and demand answers. It'll look as though you've been kidnapped rather than gone into hiding."

Trust her grandmother to see the situation clearly. "I won't be able to contact anyone in the family, even you, Gran," she said. "No phone calls, no e-mail, no letters. But I'll somehow get word to you when I've had the baby."

"Thank you." She heard her grandmother sob. "I doubt I'll sleep a wink for worrying."

Beth had spent the next few minutes outlining her plans.

She couldn't fly, because her name would be traced to her destination. The only way out of town was to drive, except she couldn't take her own car and she couldn't rent one. A bus ticket paid in cash would offer some anonymity....

But Elizabeth wouldn't hear of it and had immediately come up with a solution. "Take my car. I'll park it in the garage under the building next to yours. You go to work in the morning as usual, but take a disguise. Some dark glasses, something to cover your hair. Change at work and use the passageway that connects the two buildings. I'll leave my car on the second basement level. You have a set of keys to it, don't you?"

Beth was astonished. Her grandmother had thought of everything. "The set you gave me in case you ever lost yours?" Beth had laughed. "No chance of that steel-trap mind forgetting anything, Gran."

"Thank you, darling. I'm only happy I can help."

"And what will you drive? I'll be gone for months. I can't return the favor and let you use mine."

"I have your grandfather's old truck to get around in. I'm sure he'd appreciate seeing it get used."

Her grandfather had died five years earlier and Gran had been unable to part with any of his possessions.

"I'm getting dressed now," Elizabeth said, breaking into her thoughts.

"But it's barely dawn!"

"I need to get there before they put a watch on your building. That snake Hennessey is bound to have people stationed everywhere. We need to be careful. I'll leave my car and take a cab home."

"Gran," Beth said urgently. "Be careful! If something doesn't seem right, just keep driving. I'll figure out what to do."

"I'll be fine, darling. I'm looking forward to outsmarting a bunch of dirty cops. I never did like that Marcus."

No, Gran hadn't ever really warmed to him. If only Beth had confronted her about it, Elizabeth would have told her why. If she'd heeded her grandmother's instincts about Marcus, perhaps she wouldn't be in this situation now.

She experienced a grim satisfaction that she'd kept her maiden name.

"I love you, Gran," she said, her voice breaking.

"I love you, too, darling. Take care."

Her grandmother had hung up before they both burst into tears.

It took Beth an hour to collect her thoughts about what she had to do and to prepare for her day. She showered and dressed in one of her work suits. After packing a change of clothes and some toiletries in her briefcase, she grabbed her trash and headed out her front door.

Her eyes, hidden behind dark sunglasses, scanned the street as she walked to the trash can at her front gate. Opening the lid, she dropped the garbage bag beside the can and bent down to pick it up, lifting a piece of turf with the toe of her shoe as she did.

The key was still where she'd hidden it.

With trembling fingers, she retrieved it, then stood with the bag, flipped the turf back with her shoe and dropped the trash into the can, along with her wedding ring.

The key concealed in her hand, she crossed to her Lexus and backed it out of the driveway. "You bastard," she muttered, passing the vehicle parked farther up the street, glad she'd gone through the charade with the trash. Morgan pulled out and followed close behind her.

A half hour later, Beth turned into the underground

garage of the building that housed the architectural practice she worked for.

At the ATM located inside the building, Beth was about to withdraw all the cash she could from several of her credit cards, but then she noticed, apart from people rushing to work and the obligatory security guards, several people loitering in the lobby. They didn't look as if they belonged there. Suspecting they were plainclothes cops posted by Hennessey, she detoured to the elevators and rode up to her floor.

Heart racing, she exited, took the stairs down to the next level and hurried to the ladies' restroom, intending to change into the disguise she'd brought. How the hell was she going to escape now? She only had about one hundred dollars cash, and she was positive Hennessey would put a trace on her credit cards. If she withdrew a large sum, he'd know she was on the run.

Walking along the corridor, she noticed the cleaners' room door was open and there on the shelves were some uniforms. What could be better than disguising herself as a cleaner? She'd be invisible. Beth dashed inside, grabbed a uniform and took the stairs down to the next level, where she used the ladies' restroom to change.

Concealed inside a stall, she wound her long, distinctive blond hair onto the top of her head and fastened it, then covered it with the cap provided for cleaners, pulled the bulky uniform over her clothes and changed into flat shoes. After washing off all her makeup at the sink, she put on a pair of rubber cleaning gloves. Then she placed her briefcase in the trash and lifted both briefcase and plastic trash bag out of the can. She took the stairs all the way to the first floor. Unseen, she slipped past the security guards in the lobby and entered the walkway that connected her building to the one next door.

She rode the elevator to the garage and, after locating her grandmother's car, got in, started the engine and reversed out of the space. At the exit onto Wiltshire Boulevard, she stopped and checked to see if Morgan had noticed her.

Despite the early-morning heat of an L.A. day, her fingers turned to ice on the steering wheel when Morgan glanced up at her. Then, apparently satisfied that it wasn't Beth or her vehicle, he went back to his newspaper.

Beth let out her breath and blended into the traffic on Wiltshire Boulevard. Soon she'd join the maze of freeways that wove through L.A. and head west, far away from California. But first she needed to stop at the bank and retrieve some money from the safety-deposit box, enough to live on for the next several months.

She was cautious when she entered the bank, expecting to see more of Hennessey's henchmen. But she saw nothing out of the ordinary. Had Marcus duped Hennessey into believing the money and drugs were at another bank?

She slipped into the ladies' room and removed her disguise. The same security guard was in the vault where the safety-deposit boxes were kept. He greeted her and then, thankfully, gave Beth the privacy she needed.

She took a stack of bills, not bothering to count them, and shoved them in her briefcase, along with the notebook. After closing the box and returning it to its niche in the wall, she rested her head against it for a moment. Then, on shaky legs, she walked out of the bank, got into her grandmother's car and headed for the freeway on-ramp.

Chapter Five

Matt called himself a thousand kinds of fool as he drove back to the office, then practically bit a deputy's head off when he asked where he'd been. "None of your damned business!" he snapped and strode into his office, imagining the looks his staff must've exchanged at his outburst. He never, ever, lost his temper with anyone. It must be Beth who had him so tied up in knots. And Luke, the nosy, interfering busybody!

Matchmaking. Why on earth had he even come out with such a dumb confession? Beth must be horrified to know that was what Luke was trying to do. And then he'd been rude to her about Sally when she'd asked an innocent question about his family.

IT WAS AFTER SIX when Matt left his office and climbed into his vehicle. He didn't feel like heading home to his apartment and dinner alone, and neither did he feel like rolling up to Luke's to share dinner with him and the girls. The welcome mat was always out at Two Elk Ranch, but after his altercation with Luke this afternoon, Matt wasn't in the mood for more of his brother's meddling.

He turned toward Silver Springs, needing to talk to Beth, to apologize for his behavior this afternoon. And his brother's.

When he knocked on the door to her room, there was no answer. He pushed it open to find the bed empty and no sign of Sarah's crib.

"Sheriff O'Malley?"

Matt spun around to face one of the maternity-ward nurses.

"Are you looking for Beth?"

Please tell me she hasn't left, Matt wanted to beg her. Instead, he nodded curtly.

"She's in the solarium. It's down the end of the hall." She pointed in the direction, but Matt was already halfway there before she'd finished speaking.

He found her sitting on a sofa reading a book, her legs curled under her. He wanted to pull her into his arms; she seemed so delicate and so alone.

She glanced up at his approach and when a smile lit her face, Matt's spirits rose. "Hi," she said almost shyly. "What are you doing here?"

Matt didn't answer her question. "Are you leaving?" he asked abruptly, indicating her slacks and loose shirt.

"I got tired of sitting around in night wear. It made me feel like an invalid." She gestured at the lounge decorated with plants and comfortable chairs. Several patients were talking with visitors. "It's nice in here, so I thought I'd escape from my room for a while."

The tension eased from Matt's shoulders. At least he'd be able to spend more time with her. He hoped she'd learn to trust him.

"Where's Sarah?"

"You *are* full of questions! She's in the nursery. Take a seat," she said, nodding at a chair.

Matt pulled it closer to her and sat down. He rested his arms on his knees, clasped his hands and leaned toward her. "I came back to apologize for being so rude to you earlier today."

"There's no need. I was being far too nosy."

Uneasy at her admission, he said, "There *is* a need to apologize. You asked me a question today and I walked out on you without answering it properly."

He scanned the room. The rest of the occupants were engaged in their own conversations. What he had to tell her was so very personal and he didn't want anyone else hearing it.

The knowledge that if he hadn't been so diligent about his job, he could've saved his wife and baby haunted Matt. How could he tell Beth about the guilt that had been eating away at him all these years? How could he admit he felt unworthy of anyone's love and couldn't trust himself to love again?

But Matt knew that if he didn't talk about it, he'd never be able to move past it, never be able to have another relationship. For the first time in three years, he'd felt desire for a woman, and it was so intense he couldn't ignore it. Couldn't shut himself off from the world—from love—for the rest of his life.

"It's...difficult for me to talk about...even now." Matt could hear his voice wavering. He took a deep breath to steady himself. "My wife...Sally, was killed by a hit-and-run driver three years ago. She was seven months pregnant."

"Oh, Matt." Beth extended her hand.

He flinched when she touched his shoulder. He didn't deserve anyone's compassion. Or love.

"It's all right, Matt... You don't have to tell me any more," she whispered.

He shook his head. "I *need* to." Then before he could talk himself out of it, he said, "The driver didn't stop. At

least, not until he ran through a shop front on Main Street."
His hands clenched into tight fists and his knuckles turned
white as he fought the revulsion, the stark memories. "I
was heading home when I saw it happen and went to help.
While he was being cut out of his vehicle, a call came that
a pedestrian had been hit on the road to my place."

Matt stared at the floor. "Sally lay by that deserted country roadside for nearly an hour before someone noticed
her."

FINALLY, HE LIFTED pain-filled eyes to hers and Beth's
heart tightened at the misery she saw reflected there. "She
and my baby died a slow, painful death—while I held the
hand of a drunk driver and told him everything was going
to be okay."

His voice broke. "I...failed the two people I loved most
in the world."

"Oh, Matt." She reached out to clasp his hand.

What words could offer comfort after such a tragedy?
But words were necessary, some affirmation of his value
as a human being. As a man.

"I don't know what to say," she said softly, resisting
the urge to wince when he squeezed her hand tightly. He
needed her support, just as she'd needed his the night Sarah
was born. "*I'm sorry* seems so...inadequate. I can't begin
to imagine how you must've felt when it happened. But I do
know you would've made a wonderful father, Matt. You're
so good with Sarah."

Her heartfelt words were rewarded when his features
relaxed a little and he gave her a crooked smile. "I'm sorry,
I shouldn't have burdened you with that." He stood, releas-
ing her hand in the process.

But Beth wasn't about to let him leave. His tragic confession couldn't have been easy for him and, right now,

Matt needed all her compassion. She caught his hand again and drew him down to sit beside her on the sofa. "I didn't intend to bring up sad memories for you."

He pulled his hand from her grasp as though he wanted to put some space between them and smoothed an imaginary crease from the trousers of his uniform. "I needed to tell you. I've never talked about it to anyone except my family."

She sighed and looked out the darkened windows of the solarium. "I hated not having any brothers or sisters. It was so lonely. You're fortunate to have so much support."

"You can still be lonely in a big family."

She glanced back at him. His words held a note of heartache Beth didn't understand. It didn't seem possible to be lonely with so many brothers. He and Luke seemed close, regardless of their bantering. Becky had sung Matt's praises, telling her how much his nieces and nephew loved him. Matt O'Malley was a puzzle.

Tonight, he'd shared something deeply personal with her and Beth couldn't help wondering, *Why me? Why now?*

"I'd better be going," he said, standing again. "I'd like to stop by tomorrow and visit you and Sarah, if that's okay."

The thought of seeing him again filled Beth with a cautious pleasure, but she had to make the break before she allowed herself to rely on Matt too much.

He had the potential to destroy everything she'd worked for over the past months—her anonymity and the relative peace of mind that went with it. "Thank you but that won't be necessary. I'm going home tomorrow," she said, then wanted to bite her tongue for revealing her plans so hastily. The man's presence was making her forget herself.

"To Denver?"

She recovered her composure, stood and started

walking toward the hallway that led to her room. He was never going to find out where her real home was, tucked away in the hills outside Spruce Lake. "Yes. I'm taking the bus."

"I could give you a ride into Denver," he offered, striding beside her, making her feel closed in, a captive.

"No!" she blurted. "I mean, that's a lovely gesture, but you've done more than enough for us already. The bus will be fine."

And now he was giving her one of those looks that said he doubted every word she'd ever uttered.

"I'd like to," he insisted. "A bus is no place for a baby."

Beth paused outside the door to her room. He wasn't going to take no for an answer. "All right, thank you," she said, knowing that by the time he turned up in the morning, she'd be long gone.

He smiled, and guilt filled every one of her pores. "When would you like me to come for you?"

"How about eleven?"

"Eleven is fine." He reached into his pocket and took out a card. "Here's my number. If you want to leave earlier or you need me for anything, just call. Anytime."

"I'll do that. Thanks." Beth slipped his card into her pocket and walked through the door he held open for her. "There's my little girl," she cooed at the sight of Sarah.

"She's hungry," the nurse said. "I was about to get you."

Beth made herself comfortable, then picked up her baby. She couldn't look Matt in the eye. The lies she was telling him were more than she could bear, but her life and Sarah's depended on them.

"I'll see you at eleven, then," he said and left the room.

"YOU NEED TO COMPLETE this paperwork." One of the hospital admitting staff had shown up not long after Matt's departure and handed Beth a sheaf of papers. They were identical to the papers Beth had received earlier and placed in her top drawer, intending to deal with them later—like after she'd left the hospital.

"Can I do this tomorrow?"

The woman looked at her watch and said, "It's really important. We need your insurance details so the bill can be taken care of, and you need to register your daughter's birth-certificate details."

"I…don't have insurance. I'll be paying cash."

The woman pursed her lips. "I see," she said enigmatically and swept out of the room.

Beth pondered the fact that she was lucky she was in a smaller hospital where, until now, monetary matters hadn't taken precedence over patient care. She'd gotten away with ignoring these papers once, but this officious woman wasn't likely to let her shut them away in her bedside cabinet again.

The woman returned several minutes later. "I've checked with our accounts department. They'll accept a credit card."

Which was exactly what Beth *didn't* want to hear. Someday, she'd repay the hospital bill—with interest—but for now she couldn't risk being traced by Hennessey. If she did pay in cash, such a huge amount would raise suspicions. And there was no way she'd make an insurance claim. It'd lead Hennessey straight to her.

"Would it be okay if I settled everything in the morning, when I leave?" she asked.

"Fine." The woman sighed. "But in the meantime, you'll need to complete the paperwork and the Registration of Birth forms. I've been told not to come back without them." She glanced at her watch again. "I hate to press you, but the office is closing and I have got to get home to my children."

"I'm sorry," Beth said with as much sincerity as she could muster. "Please sit down. I won't be long." She picked up a pen and mulled over the Registration of Birth forms. Since these would be going into a sealed envelope, Beth filled them out using her real name, but balked at naming Sarah's father. It just didn't feel *right* naming Marcus as the father. He hadn't wanted a baby, and her pregnancy had caused a rift between them months before he was gunned down on the streets of L.A. More significantly, his criminal activities had put her and Sarah in danger. He didn't deserve the title of "father." Under the circumstances, Beth wasn't sure she'd ever be able to admit Sarah's real paternity to her daughter.

She chewed on the end of the pen. Leaving the space blank didn't feel right, either. She tried to think up an imaginary name, but couldn't come up with anything that sounded suitably heroic.

The woman coughed, reminding Beth that her time was limited.

The gift card dangling from Matt's flowers caught her eye. It read *To Beth and Sarah, with my best wishes, Matt O'Malley.*

Matt O'Malley. It sounded *safe,* solid and…heroic. He'd exhibited many of the qualities she'd want in a father for Sarah. He was caring, protective, capable and had treated her daughter almost as though she were his own.

Yet Marcus, her sweet little baby's real father, hadn't even wanted her!

Matt had been more of a father to Sarah in the past two days than Marcus probably would've been in a lifetime. In bold letters, she wrote *Matt O'Malley,* experienced a momentary pang of guilt, then immediately dismissed it. She could weave a wonderful tale for Sarah around the name Matt O'Malley. Her daughter would never need to know about Marcus. Never need to find out how he'd betrayed her. Betrayed them both.

That done, she placed the form inside the envelope provided and sealed it, then filled out the other paperwork, using fictitious details and hoping no one inspected it before morning.

"I'm sorry I kept you waiting," Beth said. "I didn't realize it was so urgent."

The woman practically snatched the papers out of her hands and, without another word, left the room.

Beth put a call through to Hank, the man she rented her cabin from. She'd found a card on the notice board at the local supermarket advertising the cabin for a minimum six-month rental. It sounded perfect, and when Hank offered a grocery delivery service, meaning she could hide out at the cabin indefinitely, she'd taken it. Ensuring his silence by promising him a ten-thousand-dollar bonus if he kept her whereabouts secret, she'd told him she was an author who needed seclusion to complete her manuscript. Hank had been impressed and eagerly inquired if he could be a character in her book.

Beth looked forward to getting back to the safety of the cabin. She'd set up a nursery for Sarah, having ordered most of the baby equipment online and assembled it herself. Other items she'd picked up on visits to an ob-gyn in

Denver—one who'd been more than happy to accept cash payments and not ask too many personal questions.

After arranging for Hank to meet her at the bus transfer station down the street, she packed the small duffel bag she'd bought in the hospital shop earlier that day and created a comfortable nest for Sarah in the bottom.

After a long, soothing shower, Beth fed Sarah and then placed her sleeping baby in the duffel bag, careful to leave the zipper partway open for ventilation. Minutes later, she stepped out of the hospital undetected, mingling with a group who'd been visiting another patient.

Chapter Six

Matt didn't want to believe what his eyes were telling him.

The room was bare. The bed had been stripped, the flowers gone, the crib empty.

In the vain hope that Beth was waiting downstairs for him, he ran down the stairs leading to Reception.

She wasn't there, nor was she waiting outside in the sunny but freezing winter morning.

He'd arrived early to make sure he caught her in case she planned to slip out early. Beth had acted strange when he'd insisted on giving them a ride, and he'd been suspicious of her easy acquiescence. Too bad his suspicions had been correct. He cursed himself for letting his guard down.

After checking the canteen, he approached the hospital receptionist and asked her to page Beth. "I thought I recognized you, Sheriff O'Malley," she said. "We found this letter for you in her room."

Matt tore open the envelope and with a sinking heart read the neatly written words.

Dear Matt,
I decided to take the bus, after all. Sarah woke early this morning so I felt it was best to leave when she

had a full stomach and would sleep through the trip.
I didn't want to disturb you too early. Thank you for
your offer of a ride and for everything you've done
for us both. I'll never forget you.
Kind regards,
Beth

Matt stared at the note, hoping the words would change
if he looked at them hard enough. He screwed up the note
and tossed it in the trash. He had no idea where to find her
or even where to search.

He asked for Beth's forwarding address.

The receptionist opened a file on her computer, then
looked up at him with a frown. "I'm sorry, but it appears
that the address she gave is false. And she left without paying her account. If you wouldn't mind waiting a moment,
I'll get the hospital administrator."

She made a quick call and turned back to Matt. "The
administrator would like to speak to you."

Matt thanked her and hurried over to the office. Heather
Clarke might know more about Beth's whereabouts than
the receptionist.

"Matt, good to see you," Heather said, as she opened
her office door and ushered him in.

Matt was too impatient to bother with pleasantries. "You
know where Beth is?"

Heather's raised eyebrows warned him to back off. "And
good morning to you, too, Sheriff," she said.

"I'm sorry, but I need to know where Beth is."

"We'd like to know, too. Especially since she left without
paying her bill."

Heather resumed her seat behind the desk, indicating
that Matt should take the one opposite her, then opened a
folder. She withdrew a sheet of paper and passed it to him,

saying, "I thought you might like to settle the debt, since she's named you as the baby's father."

Matt stared at his name printed neatly beside the word *Father*.

What the hell? He frowned up at Heather. "I haven't got a clue why she did this."

Heather smiled mysteriously. "I can think of a few reasons a scared young woman would want to name you as her child's father."

Matt didn't have time to question her cryptic remark. He needed to find Beth. "You knew she was scared?"

"No. I didn't meet her, but Carol was very distressed when she came on duty this morning and discovered the room empty and two notes on the bedside cabinet. One for you, one for her."

"Did Carol's note say where she went?"

Heather shook her head. "I think you'll have to accept that this young woman doesn't want to be found."

TWO HOURS LATER, Matt was no closer to finding Beth.

The hospital's security cameras had shown her slipping out at the close of visiting hours with a large group. After that, she'd disappeared into the winter night.

He thought he'd hit pay dirt when the bus transfer station down the street from the hospital had sold a one-way ticket to Denver to a woman fitting her description late last night. Matt asked the clerk to call the driver but the man was emphatic that no one answering Beth's description had boarded the bus, with or without a baby.

He called the cab company, but neither they nor the local car rental companies had dealt with a woman matching Beth's description.

It was as if she'd disappeared into thin air. His mind spun with questions. Why had Beth gone to such lengths to get away from him and to cover her tracks? Who was she running from? Was Sarah safe?

Frustrated, Matt scraped his fingers through his hair. *Forget it, O'Malley,* he told himself. *She doesn't want anything to do with you, so forget about her and get on with your life.*

His little pep talk lasted all of two seconds. He couldn't get on with his life. He *had* to find Beth, if for no other reason than to ask her why she'd named him as Sarah's father.

He needed some fresh air. Maybe he should go horseback riding with Luke? Luke was reliable and levelheaded and he was good to talk things out with. Not only that, Luke had shown an interest in Beth....

He collected his jacket from the hook on the inside of the door and headed out to his vehicle. Within minutes, he was on his way to the ranch.

"WHAT D'YOU MEAN, she's gone?" Luke demanded, hands on his hips as he faced his irate brother. "What did you do to make her take off like that?"

"Maybe it was something *you* said."

"Me!" Luke yelled. "Look, if I said anything that made her leave, I'm sorry. That wasn't my intention. I liked her. I liked her a lot."

"So I noticed," Matt growled and hurried toward the house.

When Luke reached for his arm, Matt spun around. "Don't push me," he muttered through his teeth and grabbed the front of Luke's shirt. "I'm in no mood."

Luke held up his hands in surrender. "Matt! Get a grip! You're letting your imagination get the better of you. I wasn't interested in Beth. I was goading you, trying to break through that shell you've put around yourself since Sally died."

Matt felt as though he'd been kicked in the stomach. He released Luke's shirt and staggered to the porch steps, sat down and rested his head in his hands.

"That was a low blow," he said hoarsely.

Luke leaned against Matt's vehicle and crossed his arms. "It was, and I'm sorry. But the whole family's been trying to figure out how we can help you get on with your life," he explained quietly.

Matt didn't say anything for the longest time, just sucked in air and thought about what might have been. Finally he glanced up at Luke. "You talk about me behind my back." It was a statement, not a question.

"We're your family, Matt. We all love you and care about you." Luke walked over to him. "I know that how Sally and the baby died is destroying you, but there's nothing you can do now, Matt. Hell! There was nothing you could've done at the time. Nobody saw it happen, so it wouldn't have been reported any earlier."

"If that bastard hadn't smashed into the shop, I would've been on my way home. I would've found them before it was too late."

Luke put his hand on his shoulder. "You can't know that for sure. It wasn't your fault, so don't go beating yourself up over it for the rest of your life. Let the past go," he said softly. "You've got so much to offer. Don't shut yourself off."

"I don't ever want to hurt again the way I did when I lost Sally."

Luke sat on the step next to him. "You're a good man, Matt. The best. You, of all people, have so much to give the world if only you could see it. When I heard about Beth, what you did for her...how you came through for her when she needed help…" Luke's voice trailed off. "I can't imagine the courage it must've taken for you to do that, considering your past experience. But you put your grief and fears aside and you did what needed to be done."

Pleasantly surprised by the length and heartfelt passion of his normally taciturn brother's monologue, Matt was about to thank him, but Luke hadn't finished. "I thought it was an opportunity for you to make a new start. There was something in your voice when I phoned you that first morning—an eagerness about life—that had been missing for so long. I couldn't help wondering if Beth and Sarah were the key to your future happiness."

Matt was skeptical. "So you made a play for her yourself?"

Luke shook his head. "I wanted to see if my hunch was right. The only way I could test it, short of asking you, was to pretend I was interested in her, then stand back and see how you reacted."

"Are you satisfied with your answer?"

Luke grinned. "What d'you think?"

"I think you're spitting in the wind. The fact that she's disappeared proves she doesn't want anything to do with me." He stood suddenly as a thought struck him. "Hell! I practically brought Sarah into the world, yet I don't even have a photograph of her. Of either of them," he said and paced the area between his truck and the porch steps, trying to burn off some of his frustration.

Luke watched for a while, then said, "I won't try to console you by saying you're better off without her, Matt, because I don't think you are. Being around Beth and her baby was good for you and I believe *you* were good for *them.*"

"Yeah?" Matt smiled tightly. For the first time since he'd seen Beth's empty room earlier that morning, he felt a sense of hope. Maybe he *had* been good for them. But still, Beth had left. He went back to pacing the ground between his truck and the porch. "Your instincts about my future happiness were way off base. She didn't want me, and I'll have to learn to live with it. He bristled at the thought that Beth was so unwilling to trust him, that she'd go to such lengths to get him out of her life and cut him off from Sarah in the process.

"She named me as Sarah's father on the birth registration," he murmured.

"Excuse me?"

Matt withdrew the photocopy of the birth registration and handed it to Luke, who scanned it and whistled. He glanced up at Matt. "I'm assuming it isn't true?"

Matt scowled and Luke glanced down at the form again. "So her name isn't Beth Ford."

Matt snatched the paper from him. He'd been so shocked to see his own name there he hadn't even checked Beth's. *Elizabeth Whitman-Wyatt.* How many Elizabeth Whitman-Wyatts could there be in the States?

"Can you run a check on her license plates?"

"I will. But I need to calm down first. That's one of the reasons I came out here. The hospital wanted me to take action against her for skipping out on her bill, but I paid it instead."

"Are you *crazy?*" Luke scowled at him. "Let me get this straight. You paid the hospital bill of a woman you barely know, whose real name you don't know, who claims you fathered her child—even though you know perfectly well you didn't. Why?"

"Because it was the right thing to do." Even if he never saw Beth again, he owed her an enormous debt. Being forced to confront his deepest fears by dealing with Sarah's birth had revealed something fundamental about him. He needed to get over his grief and plan for his future. A future with a family of his own.

When Luke continued to look skeptical, he said, "Because, based on what little I know of Beth, I believe that she wouldn't have taken off without paying for a damned good reason. She didn't need any more grief and that includes being pursued by the law over a hospital bill." He shrugged. "I had the money. It's no big deal."

"Matt—"

"Just drop it. Okay?" Matt didn't need to be reminded what a fool he was being. His stomach churned whenever he thought of the danger Beth might be in. If she was running from an abusive husband, Matt wasn't sure what he'd do to the guy if he ever found him, but it wouldn't be pretty.

Luke picked up a couple of bridles slung over the front-porch railing and tossed one to Matt. "It's gonna start snowing later on. Let's go take a ride along the fences. The fresh air will clear your head. Help you figure out where to take it from here."

Matt sent him a lopsided grin. "You're that sure of me, huh?"

"You're my brother," he said simply. "I've known you for thirty-five years. What do *you* think?"

Chapter Seven

Beth had begun to regret her hasty departure from the hospital. Sarah was screaming up a storm, and she had no idea what to do with her. She'd fussed ever since they'd arrived back at the cabin late last night. And now Beth's breasts were so swollen and tender, she lamented not having included a breast pump among the items she'd purchased from the hospital pharmacy.

She'd gotten a hell of a shock when Hank told her he'd towed her car from the accident scene as he drove her back to the cabin. Just how many jobs did the man have? And he was too nosy, asking all sorts of questions. Would she be staying on at the cabin? Did she want him to get estimates on repairing her car? How was her book coming along? Did she need him to pick up any extra groceries on his next trip to the supermarket? Was her family coming to visit now that she'd had the baby? And if so, he could rent them a condo in town at a discount price.

She'd contemplated offering him a further ten thousand dollars to keep his mouth shut—about *everything*. There was still plenty of money left from the safety-deposit box, and it would be more than worth it to ensure his continued silence, but then he'd chirped up and said, "I guess you have your reasons for not wanting to talk, missy, so I won't ask you anything else. I'm looking forward to my bonus too much to pry."

Yeah. Right, Beth had thought. The sooner she was well enough to move on, the better. But how to go about that, she wasn't sure. For the moment, she was safe in Spruce Lake and here she'd stay.

Before leaving the hospital, Beth was, for all intents and purposes, just another missing person. Now she was a fugitive. Her heart pounded with the knowledge that she'd committed a crime by skipping out on her bill. But what else could she do? Return to the cabin, remove the money from its hiding place, pay Hank to drive her back to the hospital and have him wait while she handed over nearly fifteen thousand dollars in hundred-dollar bills? No wonder the woman from Admissions had looked at her strangely when she'd said she'd pay cash.

One thing was certain; Beth wouldn't be asking Hank to take her anywhere soon. He had too many connections that could imperil her safety.

The stress of her predicament weighed on her. She should've boarded that bus to Denver. She could've been there long before anyone noticed she wasn't in her room and then holed up in an apartment in Denver until it was time to go after Hennessey.

Beth glanced around the tiny cabin. Her sanctuary had now become her prison.

As soon as she was feeling up to it, she'd find another place, somewhere more secluded. Somewhere far away so Matt O'Malley would forget about her. And then maybe she could forget about him....

She hoped the note she'd left was enough to explain her not being there when he came to pick her up at the hospital. It would've been extremely rude not to acknowledge how grateful she was for everything he'd done for her and Sarah.

Sarah screamed, waking her from her musings. How she missed Matt's unflappable way of dealing with her daughter.

"Sweetie, Mommy's so tired," she cooed in a calming voice, even though everything in her was stretched so tight she wanted to shout the words at the top of her lungs. She rocked Sarah in her arms while the baby screwed up her face and clenched her tiny fists and let out another scream of fury.

Beth carried Sarah to her nursery, checked her diaper once more and put her in the crib. "This is for your own good, sweetie. And mine," she murmured as she kissed her crying infant, then forced herself to walk out of the room.

After five minutes, Sarah's wailing hadn't abated. Beth went in and patted her back and talked to her some more. Once Sarah had finally settled, Beth went back to the sofa and curled up.

WHEN THE ALARM WOKE him the next morning, Matt was relieved to have been set free from his dreams. Dreams of a scared young woman, dying in excruciating pain. He was powerless to help her, couldn't communicate with her, couldn't find out where it hurt.

It'd been a while since he'd dreamed of Sally and how she'd died, but it wasn't Sally's face he saw in the dream—it was Beth's.

"Get a grip," he muttered, disgusted with himself. Beth was alive and well and the mother of a baby daughter. And she didn't want anything to do with him.

Los Angeles

HENNESSEY SLAPPED A FILE down on Morgan's desk, causing the younger man to start. "That damned woman should've had the kid by now," he growled. "Have you found anything on the computer about it?"

Morgan looked up from his screen. "It could take a few weeks before anything gets registered officially. You'll just have to be patient."

"I ran out of patience the day she skipped town!" he snapped. "And now her mother and parents-in-law are on my back again, wanting to know if we've heard anything." He pushed away the files piled on Morgan's desk and perched on it. "They know the baby's due and want to see their grandkid."

Morgan nodded. "Understandable. Maybe we could play on that? How about if we place a false report in the national papers that her mother's been involved in an accident and is in a coma? That might flush her out."

Hennessey smacked him. "Stupid! That grandmother of hers would reveal that as a lie immediately. I can't use the press."

Morgan swore and rubbed at his cheek. "I was only trying to help. We've had their phones and Internet tapped since she left and there hasn't been one phone call, e-mail or letter from her. Either they know she's okay, or they're telling the truth and believe she's been kidnapped."

"After the mess you made of her place, what other conclusion are they going to jump to?" Hennessey paced. "We've searched that house from top to bottom and still no key!"

Morgan lifted his lip in a sneer of contempt. "Since you don't even know which bank the safety-deposit box is in, it looks like you'll never see that money or those drugs again."

"Don't provoke me," Hennessey warned and strode to the door. He turned back. "Just remember how easy it was for me to dispose of her husband. I could do you the same favor," he said, his voice dripping with malice.

Morgan shuddered. He had a feeling the promised riches hidden in that safety-deposit box would never come his way—whether they found it or not.

BACK IN HIS OFFICE after the ride with Luke and then an extended lunchtime meeting with the local police chiefs— during which all Matt could think about was Beth—he opened his laptop.

Was she still in the county? The notion filled him with hope. And with dread. Hope, because he so badly wanted to see them both again. And dread, because if Beth had gone to such trouble to cover her tracks, she didn't want him finding her.

He longed to see her, talk to her, again. He wanted to talk about *them,* explore the tiny spark he believed was attempting to ignite between them. If only Beth didn't have so many secrets, they could've gotten to know each other better. If he wasn't a cop, maybe she wouldn't have taken off like that.

One thing he did know—he was never going to get any peace until he found her.

"Jolene!" he called to the dispatcher. "Hold my calls. I have work to do."

Beth had made a false declaration on a legal document— the baby's birth certificate. He had cause to search for her.

Five minutes later, he had his answer. The car was registered to Elizabeth Wyatt of Santa Monica, California.

Elizabeth Wyatt. The name mocked him from the screen. Now at least he had Beth's phone number.

Heart pounding, he flipped open his cell phone.

"ELIZABETH SPEAKING."

The voice at the other end of the line didn't sound like Beth's. Not unless she'd aged some.

Unwilling to alert the woman to his identity, he said, "I'm looking for Beth."

There was a hesitation at the other end. "Who *are* you?" the woman asked.

It was apparent she wouldn't talk to just anyone about Beth. "I'm Sheriff Matt O'Malley from Colorado. I'm calling about her car. Does she own—?"

"Beth's been in an accident?" The fear and concern in the woman's voice were palpable.

"Yes, ma'am. But she's okay," he hastened to say. "I take it she's not there?"

"No, of course not! Please, don't ever call here again." The line went dead.

That was interesting. Could the woman be Beth's mother? They had the same first name. Obviously she had no idea where Beth was, either. But why had she hung up so suddenly? Did she not want contact with Beth? He discounted that notion immediately. She cared about her, had been concerned about her being in an accident. Just who was this woman who shared Beth's name?

Matt ran a check on drivers' licenses for California. Elizabeth Wyatt of Santa Monica was seventy-seven years old. She had a near-perfect driving record—apart from a couple of speeding tickets in her red Audi A4....

So. Beth had either stolen the woman's car or it had been lent to her. She was the right age to be Beth's grandmother.

He was tempted to call her back, but was pretty sure she wouldn't answer the phone.

There were no other Elizabeth Wyatts on record. He expanded the search and hit paydirt almost immediately. Elizabeth *Whitman*-Wyatt was a thirty-one-year-old architect from Redondo Beach. He brought up a photo taken from her driver's license.

It also brought up an APB on her, claiming she'd gone missing four months ago and was wanted for felony theft and drug dealing and was a person of interest in the shooting death of her husband, Detective Marcus Jackson. Matt did a double take as he read the screen.

What he was reading was incomprehensible. Beth a drug dealer? A thief? A potential…murderer? Horseshit! It so completely didn't fit with the woman he'd gotten to know, the scared but loving mother.

He took comfort from the fact that at least there wasn't an abusive husband in the picture. She'd been honest about being a widow, after all. But she'd been married to a cop and he'd received a police funeral with all the honors due a cop gunned down in the line of duty.

All Matt's instincts told him Beth was lying, that she'd gone on the run to protect Sarah. But from whom? More than ever, he needed to find her. He didn't want to leave her exposed, alone, without him beside her. Keeping her safe.

He tried the phone number listed, but as he suspected, it was disconnected. He couldn't put his finger on why, but he was pretty sure Beth was still in Peaks County. Maybe her car held some clues.

"Jolene, I won't be back for the rest of the day," he said, grabbing his coat. "You can reach me on my cell."

BETH WOKE TO SILENCE. She glanced toward the window. Everything was white outside. It was snowing, yet she was perspiring. The fire had gone out and the room felt cold. She stood, then sat back down and put her head between her knees to stop herself from blacking out. What was happening to her?

The pain in her breasts was excruciating. It felt as if they were burning up. She had to find her cell phone and call someone. *Anyone.*

Matt had given her his card with his direct line on it. She needed him. Needed him more than she'd needed anyone in her life. She stood more slowly this time, staggered to Sarah's room and flipped on the light. It didn't work. She tried several other light switches. Either she'd blown a fuse or the power was out.

Exhausted beyond belief, she picked up her sleeping baby and made her way to her own room and laid Sarah on the bed. She needed help. Needed to find her cell phone, which she'd left on the nightstand, recharging. It wasn't there. Fishing around, she found it on the floor and cursed. It hadn't recharged! Had she even plugged it in? Suppressing a sob, she lay down on the bed, thinking, *I'll just rest for a moment,* as exhaustion overtook her. *Rest, and then I'll be able to figure out what to do.*

She closed her eyes intending to relax. Just for a few minutes…

As LUKE HAD PREDICTED, it had started snowing heavily around midday and the plows were out clearing the roads as Matt drove toward Hank's towing yard and workshop. If anyone knew where Beth had been living, Hank would. He was only surprised he hadn't heard about it earlier, given Hank's penchant for gossip.

Hank was in his shop tinkering with a car engine. The man was a regular Mr. Fix It, sometime cabdriver, tow-truck operator and delivery man. He bore an unmistakable resemblance to a weasel. His nose was long and pointed, his teeth large and protuberant. His head was smaller than average and sat on a long neck that seemed to have the ability to swivel three hundred and sixty degrees in search of gossip. On first observation, one could be forgiven for thinking Hank came from the shallow end of the Farquar gene pool. However, his odd appearance betrayed a cunning nature. Like many of the Farquars, Hank lived in virtual squalor, yet was reputed to have millions stashed in his mattress.

Hank wiped the oil off his hands, offered his hand to Matt, then looked at it and changed his mind. "Hey, Matt. What brings you out here?"

"The woman who owns that little red sports car."

Hank swallowed, his prominent Adam's apple bobbing, and in that moment Matt was certain Hank knew a lot more about Beth than he'd previously let on. Refusing to waste any more time on pleasantries, he demanded, "Where is she?"

Hank flushed. He was no actor. "Well, how would I know, Matt?"

Matt glared. "Hank, this is me you're talking to. *Where is she?*"

"I...I can't say."

"Yeah, you can," Matt countered, then glanced around Hank's workshop. "Or I might have to get my guys to take an inventory of everything here and check it against your tax records."

As Matt had expected, Hank raised his hands. "No need for that. Everything's aboveboard."

"I'll take your word for it, *provided* you tell me where she is." Matt was losing patience. Hank had a nice little business that didn't show up in his books but everyone turned a blind eye to it. If he could intimidate Hank into thinking his side business was about to be closed down, then he would. He started to take his cell phone out of his pocket.

"She lives up off Blue Spruce Drive," Hank blurted before Matt could even flip it open.

Matt smiled to himself. Hank was a coward at heart. "Where?"

"I own a cabin up there."

"And?"

"I rented it to her for six months. She promised me ten thousand dollars at the end of it, as long as I don't tell no one about her." His face clouded. "Guess I just kissed that goodbye."

"Guess you did. Is she there now?"

He shrugged. "I took her there from the bus station. I thought she was up to somethin' when she didn't want me getting her from in front of the hospital." Hank's voice held pride at his perspicacity.

"And you didn't think to tell me that? You of all people must've known we were looking for her!"

Hank shrugged again. "Ten thousand dollars is a lot of money, Matt." Then in an attempt to moderate his guilt in failing to report Beth's whereabouts, he said, "I *tried* to talk to you about her the other day, when you asked me to get estimates on fixin' her car."

And Matt had cut him off, believing Hank was about to engage in more gossip! If only he'd listened then, he'd have known everything he needed to know about Beth. "I'll deal with the serious matter of your having obstructed justice later," he said. "But, for now, where *exactly* is this cabin?"

TWO MINUTES LATER, Matt was driving toward the mountains on the other side of town and headed up to Blue

Spruce Drive, perched overlooking the town at eleven thousand feet.

The snow was coming down so heavily now, the plows were having trouble keeping up with it. Conditions could turn dangerous by tonight.

Beth wouldn't be happy to see him, but that was just too bad. He had questions that needed answers. And the first question was, *Why did you name me as Sarah's father?*

He picked his way up the snow-covered mountain road, unable to comprehend how Beth had managed to drive down it that snowy Saturday night without going over a cliff.

He was having enough difficulty negotiating it in his all-wheel-drive SUV. There'd been power outages all over the county due to the storm, and by the looks of it, Blue Spruce Drive was still without power. Smoke billowed from chimneys of the houses set on the acreage lots he passed, indicating residents were relying on their stoves or fireplaces for heat.

He pulled in at the red-painted timber gate Hank had told him to watch for. A log cabin that looked like something out of a Christmas story sat almost surrounded by pine trees. The only thing missing was the smoke coming out of the chimney. And lights at the windows.

Fresh snow carpeted the ground, undisturbed by vehicle tracks or footprints. Nobody'd survive a day like today without a roaring fire in the grate.

Apparently she wasn't here and he had no idea where he should start searching for her now. Sure as hell, if she was still in the county, Beth would've taken pains to cover her tracks even better than before. Because now she'd know he was looking for her.

Deciding to see if she'd left any clues inside the cabin,

he climbed out of his vehicle, knocked at the front door and, when he didn't get any reply, tried the knob.

It turned and he stepped inside.

The cabin was icy cold and dark. Matt brushed the snow from his shoulders and stomped it off his boots before walking into the living room. He flicked the light switches. They were dead. The fire had burned out long ago.

Then he heard the cry of an infant. Heart hammering, he raced toward the sound and burst through a door into a bedroom. Sarah lay by her mother's side, her little arms waving frantically, her cries of distress filling the room.

He strode to the bed, picked her up and cradled her inside his jacket, next to the warmth of his body. Her face felt cold through his shirt, but she quieted as she snuggled against him.

Beth lay motionless, her face pale in the snow-clouded light coming through the window.

He sat on the bed and shook her arm. "Beth!" She didn't move. He felt for her pulse. Unable to detect anything but his own racing heart, he placed his hand gently over her mouth and nose. Warm breath covered his chilled palm and her forehead was damp with perspiration. The room was like an icebox, yet she was sweating. That could mean only one thing—she had a fever.

"Beth!" he called and shook her again, ignoring the rising pitch of Sarah's crying. "Beth. Wake up!"

Sarah's crying grew louder. He made soothing noises to her and she turned her head toward his chest, rooting around as if she wanted to suckle.

He shook Beth again with his free hand. Finally her eyelids fluttered. "Wha…?" she murmured but didn't open her eyes.

Her cell phone was lying open on the bedside table as if

she'd tried to make a call. He checked it and realized the battery was dead.

Matt contemplated bundling both of them up and getting them to the hospital, but the roads were treacherous and he didn't have any way of securing Sarah in his vehicle.

Pulling out his own cell, he punched in Lucy's number. She answered right away.

"Lucy, it's Matt."

"What's the matter? And what's all that crying?"

"I've found Beth," he said, jiggling Sarah in an attempt to quiet her since she'd given up on sucking on his shirt. "But she's in a bad way. She's sweating a lot and nearly unconscious and Sarah's starving." He wasn't in any mood to make apologies for how dramatic his explanation sounded. This was one of the few occasions in his life when he was close to panic.

"Are her breasts tender and hot to the touch?" she asked.

"How the hell should I know?" he snapped. His nerves were completely frazzled. "She's pretty much out of it."

"You could feel them."

"I am *not* feeling her breasts!" he yelled above Sarah's plaintive crying. Desperate to calm her, he cradled the phone between his ear and shoulder and did as he'd seen Becky do with her daughter, Lily. He stuck the tip of his little finger between Sarah's lips and was nearly knocked sideways by the power of the suction from her tiny mouth.

Beth finally seemed to have the strength to open her eyes.

"Ah, are your breasts tender?" he asked.

She gave a faint nod.

He swallowed. He wasn't going to ask if they were hot.

Nor do as Lucy suggested. "Yeah, I guess they are," he said into the phone.

"Okay, I'm pretty sure I know what her problem is. Can you get her into the hospital as soon as possible?"

Matt strived to keep the exasperation from his voice. "Lucy, I'm in a cabin up on Blue Spruce Drive. I don't have any way of restraining Sarah in my vehicle and Beth's in no condition to hold her."

"I'll come to you, then, but first I'll need to collect a few things. How do I find you?"

He barked out directions, yelling above Sarah's strident cries since she'd relinquished his finger.

"Gotcha. I'll see you soon," she said and broke the connection.

Matt wondered how long it would take Lucy to collect what she needed and get to the cabin. Sarah seemed fine, apart from needing to be fed but he was worried sick about Beth.

"Let's go find something to make your mom more comfortable," he murmured to the baby.

In the adjoining bathroom, he wet a washcloth, squeezed it out, then went back to Beth and placed it on her forehead. "Sarah?" she whispered hoarsely.

"She's fine. Just hungry," he assured her. "Lucy's coming. Can I get you anything?"

"Water," she murmured. "So thirsty."

"I'll be right back," he said, taking Sarah into the kitchen with him. A pacifier sat on the counter. He had no way of knowing if it was sterile, but then neither was his finger. He rinsed it under the tap and stuck it in Sarah's mouth. She quieted immediately. As she suckled furiously, he filled a glass with water and returned to Beth's side.

When he placed Sarah on the bed, she began to protest and her pacifier fell out. He stuck it back in her mouth, then slid an arm behind Beth and helped her sit up. "Here," he said. "Can you manage?"

She gulped the water greedily. "Slowly," he warned. "Take it slowly and I'll get you some more."

He refilled the glass and held it for her. She finished it and lay back on the pillows. "Thank you," she whispered and closed her eyes.

Matt tried to tell himself she looked a little better as he pulled the covers up to her chin and picked Sarah up again. "Let's get some heat into this place," he said to the squirming baby and carried her into the living room.

Five minutes later he had a roaring fire going in the grate and the cabin was starting to feel warmer. He lit candles to brighten it up, then lit the wood-burning stove in the kitchen, figuring it was probably connected to the hot-water supply as a backup. Since the baseboard radiators were stone-cold, the power must've been off for a good while.

After washing his hands, he picked up Sarah, who was screaming again, having realized the pacifier didn't contain any nourishment. A search of the kitchen for any evidence of bottles of formula proved fruitless, and she continued to complain about her empty stomach.

"Hurry up, Lucy," he urged, patting Sarah's back. He glanced out the kitchen window into the gathering darkness, willing Lucy's car to turn into the drive, then went back to check on Beth. She was perspiring even more. He freshened the cloth and wiped it across her brow and along her cheeks.

"Burning up," she protested and pushed the bedclothes down. "Cool me down. Please," she begged.

When he placed Sarah on the bed, she wailed at being separated from him.

Matt wiped the cloth down Beth's arm from shoulder

to wrist while Sarah screamed and his nerves stretched to the breaking point. The shock of finding Beth in this state and feeling helpless to do anything for her, plus the racket Sarah was making, were getting to him. He forced a calm he was far from feeling into his voice. "She's really hungry. Shouldn't you try and feed her?"

"Too sore," Beth mumbled, breathing a sigh that sounded to him like pleasure. He drew the cloth down her other arm. "Here," she said and indicated her throat and chest. "So hot."

Matt swallowed. Her gown was gaping open, revealing the swell of her breast, but he did as she asked, wiping the cloth down both sides of her throat. He closed his eyes as his hand ventured near the open flap of her nightgown.

The sound of a car door slamming had him abandoning the facecloth, lifting Sarah into his arms and striding to the front door.

As Matt stood back to let Lucy through the door, she reached into an insulated bag.

"Where's the patient?" she asked, handing over a small bottle of baby formula already prepared. "It's at the right temperature," she told him and Matt stuck the bottle in Sarah's mouth as he led the way to Beth's room. The baby's wailing halted as she suckled greedily.

"You sure are burning up, honey," Lucy said, feeling Beth's forehead. She turned her attention to Matt. "What have you given her to eat or drink?" she asked as she set up her blood-pressure machine and fastened the cuff around Beth's upper arm.

"Two glasses of water."

Lucy nodded and pumped up the cuff, reached into the insulated bag again and pulled out a cabbage. "This needs to go in the fridge."

Matt stared at the cabbage.

"Just put it in the fridge, Matt," she said. She fitted the stethoscope earpieces into her ears, then turned back to Beth.

"Come on, Sarah," he muttered, curious as hell about the cabbage. "We'd better go do what Lucy says. Otherwise, there's no telling what she'll pull out of that bag next."

He put the cabbage into the fridge, then headed into the living room to inspect the fire. Sarah finished her bottle.

"You're a greedy little piggy," he cooed.

Sarah fixed him with her wide blue gaze, released the nipple and beamed at him. Matt's heart melted, even though he knew it was probably wind that had made her smile. He lifted her for a kiss and to brush his nose against her soft cheek. "You're gonna be a beauty, just like your mama," he said. He held her over his shoulder and began to rub her back. "No spitting up," he warned and went looking for her nursery.

Lucy found him in the kitchen, warming a can of soup.

"How is she?"

"She'll be fine, Matt, thanks to you." Lucy reached up and rubbed his shoulder. "But she has mastitis."

Matt resisted the urge to clear his ears. "I thought only cows got that."

"Typical male!" Lucy said with a grin. "Nursing mothers can suffer from it, too."

The tension in his shoulders eased a little. "What can I do for her?"

"You are one sweet man, Matt O'Malley. How long can you stay here?"

He shrugged. "As long as necessary."

Lucy nodded. "Good, because she's in no condition to look after herself or the baby."

"She's *that* sick?"

Lucy nodded and opened the fridge. "For the moment. But I've given her a shot of antibiotic. She'll be pretty sick for the next twenty-four hours, then you should notice a significant improvement." She withdrew the cabbage and peeled off two leaves. "However, she'll still be weak and need lots of bed rest. I'll come back tomorrow. If there isn't any sign of improvement by then, she'll have to go to the hospital."

"Can she eat?"

"Sure. A normal diet with plenty of fluids." She pointed to the soup and said, "That's a good start."

She dug around in her bag, unpacking items. "Now, this is a breast pump. I've told Beth how to use it, but you'll need to sterilize it before the first use and then every time after that." She withdrew more things. "These are the instructions on how to sterilize it. I've encouraged Beth to use it instead of relying on formula."

Matt tried not to think of Beth using this strange contraption in the privacy of her bedroom.

Lucy handed him several empty bottles. "You'll need to sterilize these, as well. Beth can store her milk in them and they get reheated like the ones I've put in the fridge with formula. Don't use the milk in your coffee if you run out of cow's milk," she ended with a smile.

"Hardly!" And then he had to know. "Ah, why?"

Lucy laughed. "It's extremely sweet and I happen to know you don't like sugar."

"Always the comedian, aren't you?" Matt said, deadpan.

She took the cabbage leaves and headed toward Beth's room, Matt on her heels.

"And what about Sarah?" he asked, feeling unsettled at the thought of being her sole caregiver. He'd babysat his nieces plenty of times, but never been expected to look after them for more than a couple of hours.

Lucy turned and rested her hand on his shoulder. "Relax, Matt. You'll do fine. Would you excuse me?" she said and headed into the bedroom.

"Now, WHERE'S THE LITTLE darling?" Lucy asked when she returned to the kitchen a few minutes later, minus the cabbage leaves. "I'd like to check on her, make sure she hasn't suffered any ill effects."

He led her to Sarah's nursery. It had warmed up and the baby was sleeping peacefully.

Lucy unzipped Sarah's sleeper and looked her over, then turned to Matt. "She seems to be fine. I've brought a few days' supply of formula, just in case Beth isn't up to feeding her. I've explained that she should try. Feeding and using the cabbage leaves are the best way to relieve the pain."

"I'm sorely tempted to ask about those leaves, but I don't think I will."

Lucy grinned. "Just keep the cabbage in the fridge. Beth knows what to do with it."

"I didn't know you were into folk remedies."

She smiled again and said, "The coolness of the leaves relieves the heat and pain. They're also a perfect fit for the breast."

"I told you I wasn't going to ask," Matt said, while his mind filled with images of Beth's breasts cupped by his big hands instead of...*cabbage leaves.*

"Matt, this isn't the time to let your weak stomach get the better of you. Beth needs your help."

Matt bristled. "I'll do everything necessary to keep them safe and well."

Lucy nodded her approval and walked back out to the living room. "I knew I could rely on you." She glanced out the window at the gathering darkness. "I should be going."

Matt opened the front door and followed her outside. Snow was falling in fat gentle flakes. "Call me if you get stuck and I'll come and get you," he said, noticing how much snow had accumulated since he arrived at the cabin. "Otherwise, let me know you've gotten down the mountain safely."

Lucy climbed into her Jeep Cherokee. "I'll be fine. I didn't have any trouble getting up here. The plows had just been through."

"You sure she's going to be okay?"

Lucy started the Jeep. "Trust me. I'm a doctor," she said and grinned. "Take care, Matt." He closed her door. She backed up to turn her vehicle around and headed out through the gate.

Matt noted that the streetlights should've come on long ago and wondered when the power would be restored to the area. Relieved that the cabin had an alternative source of heat, he collected some wood from the pile and went inside. He called the office and told Jolene he was taking a few days off. Then he spoke to his undersheriff, Ben Hansen, and asked him to take over until he returned.

Matt stressed that he didn't want any calls forwarded to him unless they were absolute emergencies.

"JUST ONE MORE mouthful." He spooned the last drop of soup into Beth's mouth and watched as her tongue came out to lick her lips.

"Thank you," she said, her voice barely a whisper. "You didn't have to do this for me."

"Yes, I did. You were shaking too much to hold the spoon."

"I meant stay and look after me."

"It's no problem. Lucy says you're in no condition to look after yourself or Sarah." He raised one shoulder in a shrug. "It was either me or the hospital."

Matt observed her nervousness when his cell rang, then detected a relaxing of Beth's posture when she realized it was Lucy.

"She got home safely," he told her, closing the phone. "She said the power should be back soon. The workers were almost finished repairing the lines. Can I get you anything else?"

Beth shook her head. "I just want to sleep."

Matt took that as his cue, picked up the tray and stood. "I'll go check on Sarah and then I think I'll turn in myself. It's been quite a day."

Beth's lip quivered.

"Hey!" He sat down again on the side of the bed. "There's no need for tears. Everything's okay. Sarah's fine." He put down the tray and rubbed her arms. "Don't cry. Please?"

In spite of his plea, Beth's eyes welled with tears that coursed down her cheeks. Drawing her against him, Matt gently stroked her back.

"S-S…" She gulped. "Sarah could've died because I was s-so stupid!"

"Shh," he soothed. "She's fine now. That's all that matters." He drew back to look at her and immediately missed the warmth of holding her close.

She reached for a tissue from the bedside table. "You must think I'm a fool to have allowed this to happen."

"You were doing what you thought was right. A mother can't be blamed for that."

She stared up at him. "You don't blame me for running out on you at the hospital? For lying to you?"

"Hey." Matt cupped her chin. Maybe now was the time

to ask, since she wanted to talk. He exhaled and said, "Why couldn't you trust me?"

The fear darted across her face. "Please don't ask me that right now. I'm not strong enough to deal with it. I...I haven't done anything illegal, if that's what's bothering you."

Apart from naming me as Sarah's father, Matt thought, watching her fidget with the sheet in her lap. *Skipping out on paying your hospital bill. And being wanted by the LAPD.*

It just didn't fit. Beth was either protecting someone—or running from someone. The person she was protecting wasn't in doubt. Sarah. But who was she running from?

Her lower lip trembled again.

Matt's heart twisted at the fear he saw there. She was terrified, and so alone. That police report was a crock. Beth and drugs didn't fit.

There'd be time enough to question her later, but for the moment, she needed reassurance. He squeezed her hands and said, "Know this—you're both safe here, with me."

Beth's features relaxed. He looked into her eyes and stroked her cheek. "I promise that as long as you're with me, nothing bad will happen to either of you."

He felt the easing of her jaw, which had been tightly clenched beneath his fingers, saw the tension leave her shoulders.

"Thank you," she whispered.

Matt willed himself not to lean forward and touch his lips to hers, aware that such intimacy would have her on her guard again.

"Get some sleep," he said gruffly, picking up the tray. "And don't get up if you hear Sarah during the night. I'll take care of her."

"*Thank you* seems so inadequate for everything you've

done for us," she murmured as she lay back down and closed her eyes. "Good night, Matt O'Malley. You're a nice man."

Matt stood watching her for several minutes, then leaned over and blew out the candle.

THE LIVING ROOM SOFA would have to do for the night. Apart from Beth's bed, there wasn't anywhere to sleep in the cabin.

It wasn't smart to have thought about sharing her bed. He needed to burn off some of his excess energy...and rampant hormones. After making sure Sarah was still asleep, Matt got into his jacket and tried the porch light. The power was back on, flooding the entry with light. He stepped outside.

The snow had let up so he strode to the carport where the wood was stored, lifted the ax above his head and split the first log.

Chapter Eight

A half hour later, he'd built up a sizable pile of firewood and was feeling bone-weary. After stacking several loads beside the fireplace, he stripped off and walked into the bathroom.

It was a two-way bath, accessed from Beth's bedroom and the living room.

Stepping under the shower, he gasped as the icy needles pricked at his skin. Once the cold water had refreshed him, he turned it to warm and rinsed his clothes. Until he got a clean change of clothing, this would have to suffice. He toweled off, then wrapped the towel around his waist and walked back out to the living room.

After setting his wet clothes near the fire to dry, he called his brother Will, asking him to stop by his place and pack some clothes and toiletries, then bring them to the cabin in the morning. He could trust Will to keep Beth's location a secret.

He fixed himself an omelet for dinner, then cleaned up and went in search of extra blankets and pillows and made up a bed on the sofa. Clasping his hands beneath his head, he stared at the firelight flickering across the ceiling and considered his situation.

He'd gotten himself into a predicament, sheltering a woman wanted by the LAPD. On the one hand was his duty as a lawman to uphold the law and report Beth's whereabouts to the relevant authorities. On the other was his need to protect her and care for Sarah. Despite all the information the APB supplied—the incriminating allegations—Matt found them hard, if not impossible, to believe. Beth wasn't a criminal.

She was scared witless and lying to protect herself and Sarah—to the point that it could've cost them their lives. If not for Beth's having named him as Sarah's father and the lucky chance that Hank had rented her this place, he shuddered to think what might have become of them. They couldn't have survived the night in a frozen cabin, Beth sick with fever and Sarah famished.

He suspected someone was framing Beth and he aimed to find out who.

A CRY FROM SARAH had him up and pulling on his still-damp shorts as he raced toward her room before she could wake Beth. "Hey, sweetie, what's the matter?" he asked as he picked her up. Her sleeper felt damp all over and her diaper— Matt held his breath and dealt with cleaning Sarah, then remade her bed, relieved that he hadn't passed out in the process.

"I think you could do with a bath, too, huh?" Matt said as he stepped back to where she lay on her change mat on the floor. He carried Sarah to the living room and placed her on the sofa and barricaded her with pillows. "Now wait there, sweetie," he said and went off to collect towels, a clean diaper and a change of clothes.

"Here I am, back again," he said as he returned to the living room. "Can you wait while I get your bath, darlin'?" He filled her plastic baby bath at the kitchen sink, checked the temperature and brought it to the living room.

Sarah started to fuss. "Hey, now. That's no way to begin

a big adventure," he chided softly. Taking her in his arms, he sat on the floor with his legs stretched out on either side of the tub.

Laying her facedown along his left arm with her head nestled in the crook of his elbow, he lowered her into the tub, making sure her face stayed above the water. It was a bathing position favored by his nieces as infants. The sensation of being in warm water had the expected calming effect and Sarah quieted immediately.

"There, isn't that nice?" he asked and rubbed her back with a facecloth in long, soothing strokes. Sarah made funny little movements with her legs.

"So, you want to be a swimmer? Okay, let's see how you are at the backstroke." He rolled her onto her back, supporting her head above the water and let her kick for a while. Then he rinsed another facecloth and wiped her face. "You've got a head start," he observed, chuckling at his pun. "Bald heads are all the fashion in the pool. Only on the guys, but you could begin a new trend."

"She's not bald."

Matt looked up. Beth was leaning against the bedroom doorway.

"Are you okay? Can I get you anything?" he asked, torn between rushing to help Beth and keeping a firm grip on Sarah, who was kicking vigorously.

"I'm fine. I heard you talking to someone out here." She sat on the sofa and reached out to tickle Sarah's foot. "I didn't realize the conversation was so one-sided."

Matt squeezed out the cloth and wiped under Sarah's chin. "It's not one-sided at all. She's been telling me what a great swimmer she's going to be."

"I heard you telling her she was bald." Beth's voice held amusement.

Matt beamed at the baby, who was smiling up at him,

and his heart did a flip-flop. "Okay, you've got long, sun-kissed locks like your mom," he corrected, then looked closely at the fair down covering Sarah's head. "At least, one day you might."

"I'm almost afraid to bathe her," Beth admitted. "I hadn't mastered it at all before I left the hospital."

"It's not hard once you get the hang of it." He rolled the baby onto her stomach again, resting her head along his arm the way he had before, and Sarah stopped kicking and closed her eyes. "See? She trusts me." *Which is more than her mother does,* he thought ruefully.

"I told you I'll keep you safe," he said quietly. "Both of you."

WARMTH SUFFUSED BETH. *Safe.* How good would it be to feel safe again? *Could* she trust Matt to keep that promise? She wanted to, so very much.

He emanated strength and virility. His cheeks and chin were covered with a dark stubble; his bare chest, wide and well-muscled, was covered in dark hair. And his arms were the kind of arms a woman would want around her, protecting her, loving her, closing out the world until there were just the two of them.

Physically, Matt was the opposite of Marcus. Marcus had been fair and always impeccably turned out. She'd rarely seen him with a five-o'clock shadow, and his chest, although well-muscled, was smooth and hairless.

Matt was everything Marcus hadn't been, in both looks and temperament. Marcus had an edge, a restless energy, that had sometimes bothered her. Matt was calm, reliable. He hadn't panicked when her world was falling apart, when she was so afraid she'd give birth beside the highway, no one around to help. No one to take care of her baby.

She gave herself a mental shake. What was she thinking?

She had no business feeling attracted to Matt O'Malley. She wasn't even sure why she'd allowed him to stay once Lucy had gone. Except that she needed him, needed him to look after Sarah until she was well enough to do it herself. *And you need him to care for you, too.*

"There we go," Matt said, lifting Sarah from the tub and wrapping her in the towel draped across his lap. He wiped Sarah's face and hands with the ends of her towel, dropped a noisy kiss on her outstretched hand, then passed her to Beth.

Sarah instantly began to fuss.

Before Beth could express her dismay, Matt said, "I'll go warm her bottle."

She touched his arm, halting him, feeling the warmth of his skin beneath her fingers. "No, it's okay. Lucy said I should try to feed her myself."

"I…I'll give you some privacy, then," he said, hurrying toward the kitchen.

Beth swore the room felt cooler after Matt departed. She could have gazed at him all night, the firelight emphasizing his well-toned arms and chest. When she'd found him there, talking to Sarah, his head bent to his task as he bathed her daughter, her heart had filled with something rich and warm. Something she was tempted to explore further.

But that wasn't going to happen. Matt was a cop and she was a fugitive. They were an impossible combination.

TEN MINUTES LATER, Matt could hear Sarah complaining bitterly. He ventured back to the living room. Beth held her daughter up to him, frustration written all over her face. "*You* take her. She likes you better."

He shook his head. "She loves you. She probably just needs to be burped."

With a sniff, Beth bought Sarah to her shoulder and rubbed her back. "I've already done this. It didn't work."

"You need to thump—gently—rather than rub."

Beth patted her daughter gingerly, afraid of hurting her, but Sarah continued to squirm and wail.

"Harder. She won't break."

"She might," Beth said through clenched teeth and gently thumped Sarah's back three times.

"Told you," he said, triumphantly, when she burped.

"I should've stayed in the hospital another day so I could learn these things."

Matt shrugged and said, "You'll learn. She's asleep, by the way."

Beth kissed the top of Sarah's head and passed her back to him. "Would you mind putting her in her crib? I don't feel strong enough to carry her."

"Want something to drink?" he asked when he returned to the living room.

"Hot chocolate would be nice." She covered a yawn. "Could I have it in bed?"

Matt had a sudden image of sharing hot chocolate in bed with Beth, holding her.... "Go ahead. I'll bring it in when it's ready."

As she walked back to her bedroom, he observed the sway of her hips, her gown drifting behind her, and decided he was arranging for a nurse to come and stay in the morning.

When he took in her hot drink a few minutes later, Beth was fast asleep. Her features had lost their tenseness now that she was no longer on guard. The tiny frown that creased her brow too easily was gone as she slept peacefully, free for the moment of the fears that haunted her.

He turned off the bedside lamp and went back to the living room, where he cleaned up Sarah's bath things. After stoking the fire, he lay on the sofa, pillowed his hands beneath his head and stared up at the ceiling. *I have a feeling this is going to be a long night,* he thought—and not just because Sarah would wake him for feeds. He knew he'd have difficulty sleeping with Beth in the next room.

A BABY'S HIGH-PITCHED cry had him sitting bolt upright before he was even awake. It'd been part of his dream. A dream about a fair-haired, gray-eyed woman in trouble, running away, clutching her baby. The baby was screaming at the top of her lungs, her tiny arms outstretched. Matt rubbed his face, then realized Sarah was crying.

He glanced at his watch—two-fifteen—and wondered how long she'd been crying. "Here I am, sweetie, no need to scream the house down," he called as he hurried into her room.

Sarah was beet-red, her face screwed up angrily, feet drawn to her chest. Matt scooped her up and cradled her against his shoulder. Her cries turned into whimpers and then hiccups.

"You are one wet little girl," he chided her softly as he changed her and fastened her into another clean sleeper. No wonder mothers were always tired. Not only did babies keep them up all night, they also produced mountains of washing. Even though Sarah wore disposable diapers, he'd already created a mound of sheets, towels and sleepers. "We'll worry about all that in the morning" he said as he carried her to the kitchen.

She was hungry and impatient. He didn't want to wake Beth, so Sarah would have to make do with a bottle.

The kitchen needed a microwave oven, he decided as he waited for the bottle to heat with Sarah screaming in his ear. "Hey! I thought you liked me!"

She stopped screaming and looked at him for a moment. She seemed about to start again.

"If you don't behave yourself, sweet Sarah, I'm gonna hop in my truck and drive into town and get myself some earplugs."

Once more Sarah stopped crying, but when he didn't continue talking, her lip began to tremble.

"Okay, so you're a typical woman, you like conversation," he murmured. "Let's exchange some juicy gossip, then, huh?"

Sarah blinked and waited.

He cuddled her and prattled on about people he knew, people he'd had to arrest—like his brother Will, who'd ended up marrying the town judge. He shifted Sarah to his shoulder and checked her bottle again. It was warm enough, so he took her to the living room, sank down on the sofa and poked the nipple into her mouth. She snuggled against him and started sucking immediately.

The little darlin' just wanted to be near someone, to feel a heartbeat and hear a voice.

IT WAS STILL PITCH-DARK when Sarah woke him at five. He stumbled from the sofa to the kitchen, put on her formula to warm, then changed her.

"We're a pretty great team, you and I," he told her as she finished her bottle. She seemed in no hurry to settle down, so he stoked the fire and spread a rug on the floor for her to lie on, then collected some toys from the nursery and lay beside her.

For the next hour, her dark blue eyes roamed the room and occasionally tried to focus on the toys he kept presenting to her. "Do you wanna go to sleep now, sweetie? 'Cause Matt does." He yawned loudly. If he didn't get some sleep, he was afraid he'd end up collapsing from exhaustion. He picked her up. "We're going to sleep now, missy," he said firmly. "Little girls need their beauty sleep and grown men, well, they just need their sleep."

He stretched out on the sofa, tucking Sarah protectively against him. Within minutes, they were both asleep.

Chapter Nine

And that was how Beth found them the next morning. When she touched Matt's shoulder, he was instantly awake.

"Hi," she said almost shyly.

He moved over to make room for her. She looked vulnerable and beautiful in a robe pulled tightly around her, her hair mussed from sleep. Beth smoothed her hand over her cheek tiredly and reached for Sarah. "Did she keep you up all night?"

"No, she's been a little angel," he answered, his voice husky as he watched Sarah snuggle against her mother.

Matt left the room, making excuses about getting breakfast ready.

When he returned fifteen minutes later, Sarah was fast asleep and Beth was obviously dead tired. "You don't look very well," he said. "How about lying down? I'll change Sarah and bring her in to your room." He picked the baby up, leaving Beth no alternative but to comply with his suggestion.

At the door to her bedroom, she turned and said, "I want you to know how much I appreciate everything you're doing for us," then walked into her room before he could answer.

WHEN BETH SWALLOWED her last mouthful of bacon and eggs, dabbed her lips with her napkin and said, "*That* was delicious!" Matt couldn't help grinning.

"Would you like more?" He was lying on his side across the end of the bed, having finished two helpings sometime earlier. Sarah was tucked up against him, sleeping.

Beth shook her head. "I couldn't. I'll be the size of a house with all this inactivity. I'm used to taking long walks."

"We can take a walk when you're feeling up to it." He checked his watch. "I need to call Lucy. Is there anything she can bring you from town?"

"I think I've got everything I could possibly need right here," she said, her eyes holding his. After a moment, she looked away and reached over to stroke Sarah's hand. Matt wondered if Beth was saying she needed him.

Feeling an urge to put space between them, he stood and said, "I've got a load of washing to do."

Beth began to get up but he stopped her. "Stay here and rest. Lucy would shoot me if she knew I'd let you do any housework."

MATT MADE HIS CALL to Lucy, reported that both patient and daughter were doing fine, then asked if she could hire a nurse.

"Not at this short notice! What's wrong?"

"Everything's fine. But I thought a nurse would be a more appropriate caregiver than me."

"Don't underestimate yourself. No one would be more appropriate than you," Lucy assured him. "After all, you're Sarah's father."

He could hear the teasing in her voice. "You know that's not true."

"If you say so. Matt? I've got a room full of patients so I'll see you around four." She ended the call.

What exactly *was* he doing here? And what was he going to do once Beth was well? Betray her by handing her over to the LAPD? Hardly. Something just didn't feel right about that report. As soon as he felt she was up to it, he was going to get some answers from her. Honest ones.

BY THE TIME HE'D finished cleaning the kitchen, the wash was ready for the dryer.

He went to check on his charges, found both fast asleep and took Sarah to her crib, holding her close to his heart. Something deep inside him seemed to blossom every time he held her. What would it be like if Sarah was *his* child? Could he love his own any more than he already adored this baby? Was he so attached to her because, by caring for Sarah, he was in some way making up for what he could never do for his own child?

He placed Sarah in her crib and watched as she slept, her tiny lips forming a perfect rosebud. Was she the connection that would persuade Beth to reveal what was troubling her? Who she was running from?

An image of Beth formed in his mind, so ethereal in her nightgown, her hand held out to him…beckoning him into her room.

Was it even healthy to feel that way about someone he hardly knew? Maybe when he learned the truth and whatever she was hiding from, he'd be able to get her out of his thoughts and get on with his life.

He went into the laundry, pulled the clothes from the washing machine and put them into the dryer. When his hands closed over a pair of Beth's panties, he had to stop for a moment and take a few deep breaths. He couldn't go on like this. He finished loading the dryer, switched it on and then went out to split more wood.

DESPITE THE NEAR-FREEZING temperature, he'd worked up a substantial sweat by the time Will's truck pulled into the driveway.

Matt went to meet him before his brother could get out and invite himself inside. Will handed him a bag containing his clothes. "Your cat's run away and your plants are trying to die."

Matt cursed himself for being so preoccupied he hadn't given a thought to the stray that had adopted him a couple of years ago. Although Wendy wasn't officially his cat, no one else had claimed her, so he'd had her spayed, got her vaccinated and installed a cat door so she could come and go as she pleased. Without the cat door, she'd tried tearing up his furniture. Her independent half-wild nature suited him. He hadn't wanted to be tied down or show he cared too much about anything. And now he'd forgotten about her. Some caregiver! "I don't care about the damned plants, but I'm worried about Wendy."

"That cat's made a career out of running away at regular intervals," Will reminded him and punched his shoulder. "Buck up. I've offered Nick and his buddies a reward to find her. I'll keep you posted."

"Thanks," Matt said and grabbed his bag, preparing to go back inside. He didn't want Will asking too many questions.

"So, she's here, is she?" Will asked.

Matt turned. "Lucy told you?"

"No. But there'd have to be a darned good reason for telling Jolene to hold your calls and not being able to get your own clothes. Then I drive in here and you're splitting wood. She must be pretty special." He grinned knowingly.

"She is. But I don't want you talking about her to anyone, including Becky."

"Ah! A woman of mystery."

Matt frowned. "She's scared of something—or someone. She needs protection. Until she's well enough and I find out what she's running from so I can deal with it, I'm staying here with her."

Will clapped him on the shoulder. "Your secret's safe. Anything you need, just give me a call." He climbed into his truck. "Take care, Matt, and I'll call the minute I hear anything about Wendy, the wayward cat."

With a salute he turned out of the driveway.

Matt carried his bag inside, dumped it on the sofa and went to check on Sarah. She was wide-awake, staring at the mobile above her crib.

He carried her to the kitchen and heated a bottle of the milk Beth had pumped. That done, Sarah latched on to the nipple and watched him as she drank, her deep blue eyes boring into him as she made loud sucking noises.

When she'd drained the bottle, he said, "Now, are you gonna stay awake and play, or are you going to be a good little girl and go to sleep while Matt fixes your mom some lunch?"

Sarah's eyes drooped as if her tummy was so full she couldn't possibly do anything more than sleep.

"You're my good little girl, aren't you?" he whispered as he took her to her room and laid her in the crib.

HE PREPARED A SALAD and canned soup for lunch. Beth was sitting up when he took it in to her. "I must be improving. I'm starved," she said when he'd set the tray with a full glass of milk on her lap.

"Lucy'll be pleased," he said, then stood by the side of the bed, feeling strangely uncomfortable. "Sarah's down for a few hours. I told her to be on her best behavior while Lucy's here."

Beth smiled up at him. "You're so good with her. I wish I'd had a camera this morning to catch you sleeping so contentedly together."

Matt grinned. "That would've been nice. Sarah's a real beauty. Just like her mom."

A flush of embarrassment stained Beth's cheeks at his words. He liked that, the fact that she was surprised and maybe pleased by his small but heartfelt compliment.

She picked up her fork and fiddled with her salad. "Why do you split so much wood? You seem to be out there a lot."

Matt shifted his feet, trying to think of a plausible excuse for his compulsion to split wood at all hours of the day or night. He shrugged. "I want to make sure you don't run out."

"There was a stack of split wood already, Matt. It's not necessary for you to go out and do it in the moonlight."

Beth looked so innocent asking him what she no doubt thought were harmless questions. If she only knew the truth. He stuck his hands into his belt loops, partly to keep them from hauling her into his arms and admitting exactly why he spent so much time splitting wood. He shrugged again. "I need the exercise."

She patted the bedclothes and asked, "Aren't you going to join me?"

"I'd like nothing better than to join you in bed," he said.

Beth blinked, then her face reddened.

Matt cursed himself. His comment held a wealth of innuendo that he'd meant in jest—well, half in jest.

Embarrassed, he excused himself, walked to the front door and stepped out into the icy air.

The snow had let up for a while. He picked up the ax.

BETH WAITED, expecting Matt to return with his own lunch, but when she heard the rhythmic sound of an ax hitting wood, she gave up and ate her lunch alone.

Matt was an intriguing man. Strong, masculine, compassionate and nurturing. She was sure he hid a sense of humor beneath that somewhat stern exterior. He'd probably meant that remark as a joke, and she was angry with herself for misunderstanding.

Last night, she'd been awakened by Sarah's cries, but was too bone-weary to move. Then she'd heard Matt talking to her daughter, cheering her along while her bottle warmed, chattering in kindly tones in the living room. She'd caught snatches of his one-sided conversation. The way he nurtured Sarah softened her heart toward him even more. Obviously, not all cops were bad. Maybe she wouldn't have to move away from Spruce Lake, after all. Maybe she could trust Matt O'Malley with the truth....

AFTER FINISHING LUNCH, Beth took her dishes to the kitchen. From the window, she could see Matt lifting the ax high, then bringing it down hard on a log, splitting it in two.

He'd taken off his jacket and his T-shirt molded his muscled arms and back. She filled a glass with water, drank it down, then held the cool glass against her breast and remembered Matt blushing when she'd asked him why he split so much wood.

What *was* that about? Perhaps he split wood at odd hours to burn off excess energy. But a more likely scenario presented itself—perhaps he did it to distract himself from her. Perhaps that remark about joining her in bed *hadn't* been completely a joke. But Matt was an honorable man. Possibly the most honorable man she'd ever met.

He'd anchored the ax in the piece of hardwood he was

using to split the logs on. He stood to his full height and peeled off his T-shirt, exposing taut muscles sheened with sweat. Beth wanted to run her hands over him. *Big* was the only word that could describe him. Big and strong and capable.

Dragging herself away from the window, she returned to her bedroom and crawled beneath the covers. Closing her eyes to shut out the image of Matt, she concentrated on breathing slowly and deeply, until sleep eventually claimed her.

MATT STRAIGHTENED at the sound of Lucy's Jeep roaring up the drive. His back was killing him. So were his hands. The calluses were raw. He stacked the last of the split wood and went to open her door.

"Hi." She offered her cheek for his kiss. "How's my patient?"

"The one in there—" he indicated the cabin "—is doing fine. I'm not so sure about me, though."

Her brow puckered. "What's up?"

He turned his hands over.

Lucy tsk-tsked. "I diagnose you've been splitting too much wood." She wrinkled her nose. "You smell like a man who's been working too hard. Go on in the house and take a shower, and afterward I'll give you some salve for your hands."

Lucy had a point. Beth wouldn't find anything desirable about a man covered in sweat and wood chips. "Thanks. I can always rely on you to bring me back down to earth. Beth's in her room," he said, following her into the cabin.

He detoured to the bathroom, undressed and stepped under the shower, cursing the prickling cold spray. He adjusted the temperature to something resembling lukewarm and reached for the soap.

"BETH'S DOING GREAT," Lucy reported when he returned to the kitchen. "So's Sarah." She paused and looked up at him. "You're doing a great job caring for them. You're good for them, Matt. I hope you intend to become a permanent part of their lives."

She took his hands and rubbed the salve into them. "They need you every bit as much as you need them even if it's for different reasons."

Back in high school, Lucy had fancied herself an amateur psychologist and matchmaker. Nothing had changed. "I'd like to believe what you're saying," he said slowly.

"Don't sell yourself short, Matt. Don't keep blaming yourself about the baby and Sally. I've got a feeling that this might be your chance to put all of that behind you." She screwed the cap back onto the salve.

Matt couldn't keep from sharing his doubts with her. "Once Beth's well enough, she'll leave. She's running from something, or someone, and I can't do a damn thing about it."

"She hasn't told you any more about herself?"

He shook his head. "She's been too sick for me to question her. And besides, right now I'm not here in my capacity as county sheriff. I'm here as—" He paused. In what capacity *was* he here? Protector? Friend? *Potential lover?*

No, not lover. Though he'd like to be. He turned away from Lucy in case she could guess his thoughts. "Have you told anyone where I am? Or where Beth is?"

"Not a soul. As far as everyone's concerned, you've gone out of town for a few days. That goes for the people at work, too, of course." She picked up her bag and moved toward the door.

Matt followed her out. It was getting dark already and snow had started falling in the past half hour, obscuring the sunset.

"I've brought a baby car seat for you to use in case you need to go anywhere." She opened her rear door and Matt retrieved it.

"Thanks. I was thinking Beth might like to go for a drive sometime, or I could bring her down to you if she needs to see you again. That'd save you coming all the way up here."

Lucy climbed in, started the Jeep and lowered the window. "Give those calluses a rest," she warned. "Judging by the pile you've split since yesterday, I'd say there's enough wood to last a few years," she added drily.

She was poking fun at him but he let it ride. "Call me when you get home, okay?"

"Sure." She hesitated before asking, "I take it there's a good reason you don't want anyone knowing where you are?"

He could read the concern in her eyes, the questions she wanted to ask. But until he had some answers of his own, he couldn't answer hers. "For the time being."

"Take care, Matt. Beth's over the worst of it and Sarah's thriving. Call if you need me, okay?"

He watched her drive out the gate and turn left onto the road to town. Then he got an armful of wood and went inside to stack it by the fireplace.

Ten minutes later, his phone rang. He'd left it out in the living room. He snatched it up and glanced at the caller ID. "Hi, Lucy. Did you get back okay?"

"I'm fine."

"Great. Well, I'll call if Beth needs to see you."

"Okay, but, Matt…be careful. Bye now."

Matt stared at the phone, wondering about Lucy's cryptic remark.

He had no intention of hurting Beth. She'd been hurt

enough by someone else. But one way or another, tonight he intended to get the truth out of her.

He made some calls, checking in with work, going outside so he wouldn't disturb Beth.

When he ventured back inside, he found her sitting up in bed, nursing Sarah.

Embarrassed at having walked in on so private a moment, he was about to do an about-face and leave when he heard Beth whisper, "Please stay, Matt. We need to talk." She patted the bedcovers. "You don't mind if I nurse her while you're here, do you?"

Matt didn't have an answer; his tongue was glued to the roof of his mouth. All he could manage was a shake of his head. He sat on the end of the bed, careful to keep a safe distance between them.

Beth held Sarah over her shoulder and rubbed her back. "That's my good girl," she said and kissed her cheek before opening her gown to let the baby suckle her other breast.

Matt's mouth was dry. He wanted to be part of this, he *ached* for it. *The whole thing.* It wasn't just sexual intimacy he craved; he wanted to be a husband to Beth and a father to Sarah. Wanted them to be *his* family.

Where were these crazy ideas coming from? Would allowing himself to believe he meant anything to Beth—that they could have a future together—absolve him of his guilt?

Beth's shoulders sagged as she looked at her daughter and said, "She's so tiny and helpless, and when I think of what might've happened to her if you hadn't found us—"

"Don't!" Matt said harshly, unwilling to confront his fears. "Don't think about it." He sat on the side of the bed, rested his elbows on his knees and rubbed his face, then flinched when he felt her hand on his back.

"What's wrong?" she asked.

"Thinking about it…tears me apart. Why did you do it?" he demanded. "Why did you run out on me?"

Beth closed her eyes.

"Don't shut me out," he growled. "Don't think you can shut me out by closing your eyes."

She opened them and fixed him with her gray-eyed gaze. "Would you mind putting Sarah in her crib, please, Matt? We need to talk."

He carried Sarah to her room and settled her in her crib. In such a short time, she'd become so precious to him that he couldn't imagine his life without her—without either of them. He switched off the light and returned to Beth's room.

"I've been a patient man," he said. "Now it's time for you to tell me the truth, starting with your real name, *Elizabeth Whitman-Wyatt*."

Chapter Ten

"H-how do you know that?"

"I ran a make on your license plates."

Her face was ashen. "Why? Why did you do that?" she asked, her voice shrill with tension.

"Is there some reason I shouldn't have?" He forced down the bitter taste of anger and disappointment. She was going to lie to him again. He'd been prepared to protect her to the point of sacrificing his career. *How could you let her bewitch you like this?*

Matt fought to keep his voice low and in control, when everything in him screamed to demand what she was up to. "Imagine my surprise when your grandmother answered the phone."

HE'D RUN A CHECK on her license plates and discovered her grandmother! It'd be there in the police computers for anyone to see. Someone in Spruce Lake, Colorado, was looking for her. She couldn't catch her breath. If Matt had found her so easily, *they* could, too!

Fear for her daughter overwhelmed her. "Oh, my God!" She threw aside the covers and went to stand, but Matt pulled her back down to sit beside him.

"You're not going anywhere."

"No! You don't understand. I've got to get Sarah. We have to get out of here!"

"Calm down!" he shouted, pulling her against his chest and wrapping his arms about her, as if trying to cocoon her from harm. "No one's going to hurt either you or Sarah. Not while you're with me. I promised to keep you both safe."

Safe! That was a joke. "There was no reason to run a trace on my plates! You told me there wouldn't be any charges, considering the circumstances." She continued to struggle, needing to get her daughter and escape.

"There was *every* reason I should look for you. Starting with…why did you list me as Sarah's father on the birth registration documents?"

The strength to fight left her body at his revelation. *He knew!* She'd sealed the papers in an official envelope and foolishly assumed it wouldn't be opened until it got to a government department in Denver. "H-how did you find out about that?"

"The hospital administrator told me. I think I have a right to know why you said I was Sarah's father, when we're both perfectly aware that I'm not."

Beth didn't want to put Matt in danger. Telling him the truth would do just that.

"I can't. Please leave it at that. I have to go. And I don't want you following me."

Again she tried to get up and again Matt pulled her down. "I've had enough of you running out on me. If nothing else, you're going to tell me why you named me on those documents, instead of your husband."

She flinched at his harsh command. Matt was right; he deserved an explanation. "Okay, but you're not going to like it," she warned. "I couldn't put my husband's name because I'd discovered Marcus was a dirty cop. He was shot four months ago by another policeman."

No wonder she'd been so wary of him from the start. He knew her husband was a cop. But was she saying the shooting wasn't accidental?

"You'd better tell me the whole story—from the beginning."

Beth raised pleading eyes to his, and he detected the unshed tears she was trying to contain. "You don't know them. They won't give up until they've found me! Please, *please* let me go."

Matt tightened his grip on her. "*Who* is looking for you? Who could possibly want to hurt you?"

"I can't tell you! They'd kill us all."

Feeling as though the air had been punched from his lungs, he loosened his grip on her. *Kill?* Just what kind of trouble was she in?

Taking advantage of his momentary lapse, Beth managed to shuffle away from him toward the headboard and sat with her arms protectively around her knees.

She seemed so forlorn, so scared. He reached out to clasp her hands. They were icy. She stared wide-eyed at the door as though expecting someone to come in at any moment. Either that, or she was thinking of other ways of escape.

"Look at me," he urged, his voice gentle with compassion.

Beth tore her gaze from the doorway and focused on him.

When he knew he had her attention, he said, "I made a promise to you and I *never* break my promises. I will protect you with my life, but to do so, I need to know the truth. *All* of it." He drew her into his arms and held her against his heart.

He waited, breath held, praying she wouldn't feed him any more lies.

Finally her shoulders relaxed. "I've tried so hard to keep us safe," she whispered, then pulled back and looked up at him. "You're not going to like what you hear," she warned.

"As long as it's the truth, I can deal with it."

She took a deep breath and launched into her explanation. "Marcus—my husband—was working undercover. He was shot during a drug bust.

"I thought it was an accident—or that's what I was led to believe, that he'd been mistaken for one of the gang they were after. The LAPD gave him a full police funeral. But when his former partner and another cop broke into my house and threatened me later that night, I realized it wasn't an accident."

What Beth was telling him was so far from what he'd expected her to say. His suspicions raised about the APB, he asked, "What's his partner's name?"

She frowned up at him, as though gauging whether it was safe to admit the truth. "Detective John Hennessey."

Hennessey! The contact name on the APB. So, his skepticism about its contents was correct.

"They thought I knew where Marcus had hidden their cache of drugs from a big bust and a great deal of money, too." She paused, shaking her head. "My husband was a dirty cop. We were married for five years and I had no idea."

"I don't understand why you believed so easily he was corrupt? Just on their say-so?" Surely she wasn't that gullible.

When Beth explained how she'd found the key and used it at the bank—and told him about the money she'd discovered in the safety-deposit box—Matt conceded that it did indeed look as if her husband was a crooked cop.

"Hennessey wanted the key. I pretended I didn't know anything about it. They trashed my house and told me if I reported them, they'd kill me…and my baby." She took a deep breath. "I did the only thing I could. I ran. And up until now, I was safe here in Colorado."

Until he'd done a trace on her license. Matt cursed himself, wishing he could take it all back.

"Why Colorado? Why *here* in Colorado?"

"I came here on a ski trip during college. I liked the town. It felt safe, secluded from the outside world. I thought as I was driving east…" She paused. "I didn't know where I was headed when I left L.A. I only knew I needed to get out of there and fast. In Arizona, I saw a news report that I'd gone missing. Fortunately I was wearing a wig and no makeup, so the picture they showed on the TV news didn't bear much resemblance to how I looked. I had to get away from the interstate, so I took back roads going north and ended up in Colorado. That night while I was scanning the map, searching for where to drive next, I saw Spruce Lake and remembered how much I'd liked it. I decided to come here, get a room for the night, see if I felt the same way about it."

"And you did?"

She nodded. "I saw an ad at the supermarket for a place that sounded perfect. I met the owner here, loved the cabin's charm and seclusion. When he said he could provide a grocery delivery service at a small additional charge, I was sold."

She frowned as something occurred to her. "I've never asked, but how did you find me here?"

"I went to Hank's, intending to look through your car for any clues as to where you might've gone. Hank told me."

"He sold me out?"

"Not without a bit of persuasion, mostly pertaining to his tax records."

She snorted with contempt. "I told him I was an author and needed complete privacy to finish my manuscript and offered him ten thousand dollars to keep my whereabouts a secret. Needless to say, he won't be getting his 'bonus' now."

"If he sold you out for a lousy ten grand, that might be an indication of how much more he isn't reporting to the IRS." But this was only part of the picture and Matt needed to know more. "Tell me, how does your grandmother fit into all this?"

"Have you spoken to Gran?" she demanded, the fear returning to her voice. "How is she?"

"I don't know. She told me never to call again before hanging up."

"Oh, my God! Don't you get it? They've tapped her phone!" She struggled out of his arms again, but Matt brought her back.

"Calm down," he said. "If you'd been honest with me in the first place, I could've protected you from the start."

"How could I trust you? I couldn't trust my own husband!"

"Do you trust me now?"

"You traced the car to my grandmother. Her life could be in danger right now!" she yelled, slapping at him, trying to escape.

Matt tightened his grip and said calmly, "Granted, but if they were recording her phone calls, they'd realize she knew nothing other than that the sheriff of Peaks County, Colorado, had called her. What's more concerning is that I did a trace on Elizabeth Wyatt and found you. According to the APB, you're wanted for drug possession and felony theft."

The color drained from her face. "Please, take Sarah, keep her safe!" she cried and slipped out of his arms.

"Whoa, there!" Matt caught her at the door. "You're not going anywhere without me. If Hennessey's responsible for your husband's death, then he'll be brought to justice."

"You've got to be kidding! This isn't a beat cop from some *backwater* in Colorado. Hennessey is a hardened big-city cop who knows all the tricks. Don't even think about going to Internal Affairs! Who knows how far his talons reach? He could even have judges on his payroll."

Matt conceded it would be more difficult to implicate Hennessey if that was the case, but there had to be a way, one that would ensure Beth's safety. "I need to ask—how did you support yourself all these months?"

"Since Hennessey had cops posted in the lobby of my building, I couldn't withdraw anything from the ATM there, so on my way out of L.A. I stopped at the bank and took as much money as I could out of the safety-deposit box. There must be hundreds of thousands still in there."

Matt whistled softly. "Okay, go back to what happened after Hennessey left your house."

Beth bit her lip as though contemplating whether it was worth it. Then she started talking.

A HALF HOUR LATER, Matt was satisfied that he understood everything. He was shocked by the stress Beth had borne all this time.

She reached for a tissue, blew her nose and said, "Sarah's safety was my main priority. But to keep her safe, I needed to completely cut any ties with my old life." She dabbed at her eyes. "It was so hard to leave my family and friends behind, not to let them know where I was. But that would only endanger them, as well." She rested her head against his chest. "Oh, Matt, I've been so alone!"

His heart nearly broke at the desolation in her voice. He stroked her back and said, "You're not alone anymore, sweetheart. You've got Sarah and me and my whole family on your side."

She looked up at him, her eyes filled with pain instead of the hope he'd expected to see there. She shook her head emphatically. "No. All I have is Sarah. And we have to get out of here before they trace me to Spruce Lake and start asking questions. If you could find me so easily, so will they."

"Relax. No one knows where you live. You've covered your tracks very well. And I have a way of covering them further."

"No!" She gripped his arms so fiercely, her fingernails bit into his flesh. "Whatever you do, please promise me you won't start investigating. They'll come after you and kill you, too. I couldn't bear it if anything happened to you! Don't you see? That's why I have to get out of here."

Chapter Eleven

Matt gazed out at the moonlit snow. The weather had finally cleared and the sky was sprinkled with glittering stars.

He'd come into the kitchen to fix them something to eat. Beth's revelations had left him tormented and confused.

On the one hand, it was his duty to report the criminal activities of members of the LAPD. On the other, he had to protect Beth. But how could he effectively achieve that without exposing her to more danger?

Damn computers! They had such an indiscriminate way of disseminating information.

If he started investigating anything to do with Beth's disappearance, it would alert the people who were after her. Hennessey would be all over them in no time.

Matt had been a cop long enough to know they'd be totally unscrupulous in their methods to get hold of what they wanted.

WHEN HE CARRIED A TRAY loaded with grilled cheese sandwiches, a soda for him and glass of milk for Beth into the living room, he found her staring into the fire. He could tell by the way she sat so erectly, her jaw tensed, her hands clenched in her lap, that she wasn't much calmer than when he'd left her there fifteen minutes earlier.

They ate in silence, Beth only picking at her sandwich. "Do you have any idea what happened to the drugs Hennessey claimed Marcus was keeping from the rest of his buddies?" he finally asked.

Beth glanced up at him. "Why do you want to know?"

"Because if there's some physical evidence of their criminal activities, it'll be easier to nail them."

Her eyes widened in alarm. "You *promised* you wouldn't pursue them!"

Matt shook his head. "I said I'd make arrangements to throw them off your trail. I didn't say anything about not going after them."

"It'll never be over, will it?" She looked back at the fire, her expression grim. "They'll come after you, Matt, and they'll kill you to get to me. They'll kill my *baby* to get to me! Sarah and I will never be truly safe."

"You and Sarah won't be safe as long as they're still out there, free to carry on their criminal activities—whether I get involved or not. I can do this discreetly." He drew his hand through his hair. "But I need evidence."

Beth looked at him for a long time, as though weighing her options. Finally she expelled a breath and said, "Promise me this won't blow up in our faces. *Promise me!*"

He nodded. "I promise."

She went to the fireplace and pried a piece of loose mortar from above the mantel and handed him a key.

"Like I told you, I found this the day before Marcus's funeral. I was curious about it because we used to have a safety-deposit box, but Marcus said he'd returned the key after we'd had a home safe installed…." She paused for a moment as if wondering whether she should reveal anything else.

"Go on," he said, suspecting that what she'd told him previously wasn't all he needed to know.

"The box contained papers, a list of names in a notebook, details of transactions and other things I didn't really understand. There was also a lot of money. And another key."

"Did you use that key?"

She nodded. "Of course I did. I was curious to know why there was money—so much money—in our old safety-deposit box.

"I needed answers to the dozens of questions racing through my mind. Where could the money have come from? Did it belong to someone else? Was there some sort of mix-up at the bank? Why was Marcus's handwriting in that notebook? What did it all mean? I *had* to know what was going on. It…it made me wonder about the real circumstances of his death.

"I didn't know what box number the key was for, so I took a guess—627, our anniversary—and it turned out to be correct. That set off alarm bells. If this was police business, why use our personal safety-deposit box? The second key opened a much larger box containing bags of white powder." She shrugged. "I'm assuming it was heroin or cocaine."

"What did you do then?"

"Do?" She looked at him, horrified. "I didn't do anything, of course! I was in shock. I needed to think and couldn't do it in the bank vault. I kept looking over my shoulder, thinking someone would turn up and arrest me for drug possession. So I left everything just the way I'd found it, closed the boxes up and went home. I tried to convince myself it must've been connected to Marcus's undercover work. I was going to turn the key in. But something—I can't put my finger on it…an instinct that this

wasn't right—told me to hang on to it. Like I said, if the money and drugs had anything to do with his police work, then why wasn't it stored somewhere official?"

"Exactly. That was smart."

She smiled at the compliment. "I'm not sure I *was* so smart. If I'd left the key where I'd found it, maybe I wouldn't have had to go on the run."

"Yes, you would, since the alternative is…you'd be dead."

She frowned at his harsh statement and he explained, "Because even if you'd never found the key, Hennessey would've had to dispose of you to prevent being exposed for what he was. *Is*," he corrected. "But if Morgan's search was so thorough, why did he fail to find the key? You said you took it home."

She nodded. "I was so overwhelmed, I couldn't think straight. The implications sickened me. I didn't want the key in the house, so I buried it in the front garden. I had to get the stress of the funeral over with before I could deal with anything more.

"But I didn't get a chance to because Hennessey and Morgan showed up and turned the house upside down, looking for it. Then they threatened me and my baby. He gave me twenty-four hours to come up with the key. *Or else*. I didn't need to be Einstein to know what 'or else' meant."

She glanced back at the fireplace and shuddered. "Maybe I should've handed it over to them. Maybe they would've been satisfied with that and gone away and left me alone— and Sarah wouldn't be in danger now!"

Matt caught her chin and turned her toward him. "If you'd handed it over, you'd have been dead ten seconds later. They're desperate men. They can't afford any loose ends. Given the circumstances—not knowing who you could trust—you did the right thing."

Beth looked as though she wasn't so sure. "I've asked myself a thousand times—why didn't I mail them back to the LAPD and let them take it from there?"

"Them? I thought you only took one key."

She nodded. "But I also took the notebook, as insurance."

"Where is it?"

"At the bottom of the woodpile under about six feet of snow."

Matt smiled. "And you were going to retrieve that when?"

She shrugged. "I was hoping…I was hoping someone would realize that Hennessey was crooked, he'd be arrested and then I'd feel safe about sending in the evidence."

Matt had to concede that if he'd been a pregnant woman whose life had been threatened, the last thing he'd want to do was risk exposing himself to anyone within the department who might be in on the corruption. "Anything else you've got hidden around here that I might need to know about?"

"Well, there's about thirty thousand dollars at the bottom of the woodpile, too. Minus a few thousand I've needed for day-to-day expenses. And I paid Hank six months' rent in advance." She pulled a face. "Just as well I stole some of that money, huh? Otherwise, I wouldn't have had anywhere to live."

So at least part of the APB was correct, since she was wanted for felony theft. Not that Matt had any intention of calling her on it.

Beth shook her head in disbelief. "I thought I loved my husband and we were happy, we shared everything. But when they came to the house and threatened me and my baby, something inside me died. It was as if Marcus had been living a whole other life—he was someone I didn't know at all. If I couldn't trust Marcus, then who could I trust? I was so angry he'd put us in such a dangerous position. So hurt and betrayed. Any love I'd ever had for him died at that moment." She squeezed her eyes closed as though she could shut out the memory. "I decided the only way we'd be safe is if I got as far away from L.A. as possible, so I packed my briefcase with a few things, dug up the key and pretended I was going to work for the day. It was just as well, because Morgan followed me."

Matt stroked her cheek. "Like I said—that was smart."

She allowed another small smile of gratitude. "At work, I changed into a cleaner's uniform and found where my grandmother had left her car for me under the building next door. The disguise and the different car fooled Morgan and I managed to slip past him."

"And you ended up here in Spruce Lake," Matt supplied as he returned the key to its hiding place, then drew her back to the sofa.

She nodded and sat down, her legs beneath her. "I loved being in the mountains. They represented the new life I'd chosen. The scenery was the complete opposite of L.A. There were wide-open spaces, endless blue skies and plenty of fresh air. The people—whenever I ventured out to do a couple of errands—were friendly. I felt…safe here."

"But you kept your grandmother's car."

"I needed it for transport and nobody traced me to it. Until I ran off the road."

"And I ran a make on the license plates," he finished for her.

She nodded, her lips pressed together. "Now do you

understand why I told you so many lies about my name, about where I lived, why I ran away from the hospital?"

Matt nodded and smoothed her hair. "So, back to my first question. Why did you name me as Sarah's father?"

"I…didn't know what else to do. I couldn't name Marcus, I just couldn't. After what he'd done, he'd forfeited that right. I didn't ever want to be reminded of him and how he'd betrayed us."

Her mouth turned up in a bittersweet smile. "You saved our lives and you were so kind to me in the hospital. I couldn't think of anyone more fitting to name as Sarah's father."

Matt felt inordinately cheered. Almost from the beginning Beth had believed he'd be a good father.

"I thought I could weave a wonderful fantasy around your name if Sarah ever asked me about Matt O'Malley. I…I'm sorry."

Matt could barely wipe the smile off his face. "It's okay," he said and smoothed a tendril of hair from her face. "It led me back to you, and for that I'm eternally grateful."

"Then you forgive me?"

Since Beth's confession, the last of his doubts about her had evaporated. Her reasons for naming him as Sarah's father filled him with a happiness that went clear down to his toes. Maybe, just maybe, she could be persuaded to trust him. Without reservation.

Matt cupped her chin and said, "I couldn't think of anything nicer than being called Sarah's dad. Except maybe this…" He placed a tender kiss on her lips and almost drowned in their welcoming warmth and softness. He held her against his heart, content for now just to hold her close—until Sarah wakened and started to cry.

"My turn to get her," Beth whispered and eased out of his arms. "Thank you for believing me," she said, her voice shaking. "It's been such a terrible burden to bear alone." And then she was gone, before he could react, before he could say anything.

Matt tried to swallow the lump in his throat as he watched her leave. He got up and went into the kitchen for a glass of water. If he could stop thinking about Beth, the woman, and concentrate instead on what to do about her situation, it might take his mind off wanting to make love to her. He sure didn't want to go out and split wood in the moonlight again.

In the living room, he stoked the fire, then paced the floor, listening to Beth cooing to Sarah in her room.

He looked at the sofa. He didn't want to sleep there tonight. Alone. He wanted to sleep with Beth, his arms around her.... *Think about what you can do with the key. The key, the key,* his mind urged, but all he got was a vision of Beth holding it up, her eyes pleading...

FIFTEEN MINUTES LATER, he was no closer to a solution, having discounted a number of alternatives. A sound from the kitchen made him instantly alert. A dim light glowed there and he strode toward it, every nerve tensed for battle.

He rounded the corner silently, then stopped short when he saw the scene before him. Beth was at the refrigerator, retrieving something from inside. The fridge light glowed through her nightgown, outlining every feminine curve.

Matt cleared his throat. Startled, she dropped the carton of milk she held.

"Oh! You frightened me," she said and turned toward him.

Matt retrieved some paper towels and bent to clean up the mess.

"I...I'm sorry. I'm not usually so clumsy," she apologized and crouched down to help him.

Her arm brushed against his, sending tentacles of awareness creeping up his spine.

He stood abruptly and washed his hands. He wanted so much to explore a relationship with Beth. But until they'd resolved the situation she was in, he needed a clear head. Getting romantically involved with Beth right now could endanger them all.

When he turned back to her, she was frowning. "What's the matter?" he asked.

"Nothing," she said too quickly, her voice husky with the tension they both felt. She licked her lips.

In two strides he was in front of her. Beth's frown returned and she backed up against the kitchen wall. She raised her chin defiantly as though challenging him to kiss her.

Matt was acutely aware of her nearness, could sense her chest rising and falling. To hell with keeping a clear head; he needed her. If he took one more tiny step toward her, her breasts would brush his chest. "What would you do if I kissed you?" he asked softly.

"I'd let you," she replied and raised her chin a little higher.

Matt almost gave in to the urge to take her in his arms and kiss her long and hard. Instead, he braced his forearms against the wall above her head and bent to touch his lips to hers.

A sigh of pleasure escaped her, urging him to deepen the kiss, and he did.

BETH WAS CERTAIN SHE'D never experienced anything so arousing in her life. And Matt was barely touching her!

He drew back a little, breaking the kiss slowly.

"Mmm, that was nice," she murmured, hoping he'd kiss her again, yet confused as to why she was feeling this way. Her hormones must be completely haywire.

He lifted her onto the counter and pulled her against him. Beth returned his passion, needing his closeness, needing his kisses and how they made her feel. Needing to feel alive. She reveled in the intimacy of their position, his hands drawing her hard against him.

Emotions were overwhelming her, making her head spin, but Matt suddenly tore his mouth from hers.

He stood for a moment, breathing deeply. "I'm sorry. I shouldn't have done that," he said gruffly and rested his forehead against hers, tracing a callused thumb across her bottom lip.

Her nerve endings tingled as he trailed his hand down her cheek and throat, his chest rising and falling as fast as hers. It thrilled her to know he was as affected by their kiss as she was.

"I have to get some fresh air," he finally said and went back into the living room.

Before Beth had a chance to collect her scattered wits, Matt had put on his jacket and boots and stepped outside in the snow.

She heard the ax make contact with the firewood and wondered what she'd done wrong. Why had he lit out of there like that?

For a long time, Beth sat on the countertop, waiting for the strength to return to her legs. When it did, she slid off the counter and stumbled back to her room. She climbed into bed, pulled the covers over her head and resisted the urge to cry herself to sleep.

Chapter Twelve

They ate breakfast in silence the following morning. Beth realized each wanted to discuss what had happened the night before, but neither was ready to broach the subject.

Finally Matt broke the silence. "Let's take a drive," he suggested. "It's my niece Sasha's birthday and I've gotta drop in on her. Then I wanted to show you something—a surprise."

Beth felt herself blanch. "I can't go out anywhere! I can't risk anyone seeing me. Not now!"

"Relax. It's only my family, and it'll do you good to get some fresh air."

Beth chewed on her lip, not at all comfortable with venturing into the outside world. He covered her hand and said, "You'll be safe. We're not going where anyone other than my family is likely to see you. Go put on some warm clothes and I'll get Sarah ready. She'll enjoy the outing as much as I'm hoping you will."

"If you're *sure* it'll be safe…"

"It will be. I promise. I can't let Sash down."

"How do we transport Sarah?"

"Lucy brought a car safety seat that I can fit into my vehicle. She also brought over one of those baby slings. I'll wear it and Sarah will be safe and snug."

"Will your parents be there, too?"

"No, Mom and Pop travel a lot since they retired and handed over running the ranch full-time to Luke. They're sailing around the Caribbean with some friends of theirs."

Beth tried not to tell herself what a relief that was. Meeting Sarah O'Malley, having her know she'd named Sarah after her, could be seriously embarrassing.

"All right," she finally agreed, reluctant and yet oddly excited, too.

MATT FOUND THAT being cooped up in the cabin with Beth was testing his resolve. Taking a drive in the fresh mountain air would clear their heads, but still keep Beth safe by his side.

After fitting the baby seat in his truck, Matt left the engine running and the heaters going full blast. He went back inside, dressed Sarah in a snowsuit with built-in mittens and a hood and put on the baby sling. He adjusted the length of the straps and slipped it on, then lifted her into it. "Perfect, my little angel, just like you." He walked into the living room where Beth was waiting.

Pleasure filled him when she grinned and said, "That's adorable. She looks so contented."

Matt wished Beth could look half as contented as he unfastened the sling, gently lifted Sarah from it and transferred her to the safety carrier, which would fit directly into the seat.

Satisfied that she was secure, he picked up the carrier and headed for the door. "Ready?" he asked and opened it for her.

BETH ZIPPED UP HER JACKET and stepped outside into the crisp air. Overnight snow carpeted the landscape beneath clear, sunny skies. The pines surrounding the cabin drooped heavily beneath their white burden.

"It's so pretty," she said, smiling as a pair of squirrels chattered noisily in the pines above them, chasing each other from branch to branch and sending showers of snow onto the driveway. "I haven't really had a chance to appreciate this."

Matt locked the front door and held her gloved hand to help her toward the car. "Is it any wonder I choose to live here?"

"None whatsoever," she told him as she climbed in, then turned in her seat to watch as Matt fitted Sarah's carrier neatly into its base, all accomplished without disturbing her sleep.

Beth settled back in her seat, taking in the scenery as Matt drove. It felt slightly surreal. She hadn't been outside in the sunshine for almost a week, yet it seemed months.

The plows had already cleared the mountain road, and Matt went at a leisurely pace. As if reading her thoughts, he said, "I couldn't imagine staying in that tiny cabin for weeks on end. I love the outdoors too much."

"Me, too," she agreed. "I'm looking forward to the day when I can go for some long walks in the snow. I think Sarah would love that."

At the bottom of the road, he made a left and headed away from Spruce Lake.

"I've never been this way before," she remarked after they'd gone about two miles.

Matt glanced over at her, a dark eyebrow raised. "It's the way to South Ridge."

Beth could feel herself blushing and reached to turn down the heater. She'd forgotten her earlier lie about having been in South Ridge to visit a client.

Matt chuckled.

"You didn't believe a word of what I said back at the hospital, did you?"

"Sweetheart, the only thing I knew for sure was that you'd had a baby and you were hiding something. Pretty much everything else was distinctly fishy."

Beth crossed her arms. "Frankly, I'm impressed at how creative I was."

He grinned across at her. "Creative…but not particularly convincing."

The valley opened up a little wider and hills rose gently toward the snowcapped mountains on either side.

Eventually the valley widened until there were several miles of undulating valley floor between the foothills. Matt turned off the main road and drove over a cattle grate. The name Two Elk was emblazoned in wrought iron above it.

A half mile farther on, he pulled up in front of a substantial ranch-style house. Even before he'd gotten out of the car, the door was flung open and three young girls came racing toward them.

"Uncle Matt! Uncle Matt!" they all squealed in unison.

Beth opened her door and climbed out, delighted by their obvious affection for their uncle. The girls were so involved in greeting Matt, they didn't notice her. She was about to get Sarah out, but Matt beat her to it. "I've got her," he said and lifted Sarah's car seat out of its base.

Beth collected the bag of baby paraphernalia and went around to join Matt. The three girls still hadn't acknowledged her as they were now scrabbling to get a look inside the carrier. "Let me see! Let me see!" demanded the youngest, who Beth guessed to be three or four.

"Patience, Celeste," Matt said. "Let's get Sarah out of the cold first." He turned to Beth and slid his arm about her waist, drawing her against the shelter of his body. "Girls, I'd like you to meet my friend Beth."

The girls all chimed, "Hi," and smiled at Beth, then went back to peeking at Sarah. Beth couldn't help laughing at their enthusiasm as Matt, his arm still encircling her waist, drew Beth along with him.

They mounted the four steps onto the porch and the door was flung open yet again. Luke stepped out, a wide grin on his face. "Hello, Beth," he said, clasping her shoulders and bending to place a kiss of welcome on her cheek. He held her away from him, looked knowingly at Matt, then back at Beth. "I'm glad to see my brother tracked you down," he said and ushered them all inside.

Anything else he had to say was drowned out by the girls' squealing and demands to hold Sarah.

Matt put the baby carrier on the living-room sofa and asked Beth, "Do you mind? I'll make sure they don't kill her with kindness."

He looked so endearing trying to fend off the girls while he waited for Beth's answer.

"Of course they can," she said and bent to pick up Sarah. She was lying awake and gazing out at the sea of faces.

"Me first!" the youngest cried.

"No, me!" the oldest yelled. "It's *my* birthday!"

Beth glanced at the middle girl who seemed the least interested in Sarah, although her eyes still shone with excitement.

"By the way, I don't think you've all been properly introduced to Beth," Luke boomed above the racket. "The little dynamo is Celeste. This is Daisy—" he rested his hand on the middle girl's shoulder "—and the birthday girl is Sasha."

"Since I haven't brought a gift to celebrate your birthday,

Sasha, perhaps I can make up for it by letting you hold Sarah first," Beth offered.

This brought howls of anger from Celeste, who immediately threw herself on the floor and started screaming. Sasha paid no attention to her sister whatsoever and stepped over her to grab Sarah.

Matt interrupted Sasha and said, "Whoa, there! How about if you sit down, Sash? Don't want you dropping her."

Touched by Matt's concern, Beth smiled at him and then waited until Sasha was settled on the sofa to put Sarah in the girl's arms.

Sasha sighed with gratitude. Daisy frowned, muttering, "Babies are dumb, anyway," and stalked out of the room. Celeste continued to make a commotion on the floor.

Matt bent down to pick her up and swung her in the air. The sobs of anguish soon turned to shrieks of delight as he spun her around above his head.

"You know you're supposed to ignore her when she carries on like that," Luke admonished him. Matt shrugged and went on spinning Celeste around.

Luke turned to Beth and raised his eyebrows. "Can I get you a drink?" he asked, then walked into the adjoining kitchen, indicating Beth should follow.

She found herself in a large country-style kitchen that looked out at the mountains rising in the distance behind the house.

"Juice okay?" Luke asked.

"Yes, thanks."

He produced a glass pitcher of orange juice from the fridge, poured two glasses and gave one to Beth. He leaned back against the counter and studied her. Beth refused to flinch under his scrutiny. Finally he said, "My brother was like a lost bull calf when you took off from the hospital without a word. Turned the whole family upside down, I can tell you."

Warmth infused her at the knowledge that Matt had been searching for her so diligently, and she felt a surge of gratitude that he'd found her. With trembling fingers, she raised the glass to her lips.

At that moment, Sasha burst into the room brandishing a fifty-dollar bill. "Look what I got from Uncle Matt, Dad!" she announced and danced around the room.

"Matt!" Luke yelled in the direction of the living room. Sasha raced out the back door and waved the bill at Daisy, who was perched on the corral railing.

Matt poked his head around the kitchen doorway, glanced back to where Celeste was sitting on the sofa holding Sarah, then grinned at Beth, giving her a wink. "Hey, how often does a guy's niece turn twelve?" he asked. "Also it helped bribe her into letting Celeste have a turn with Sarah," he whispered.

Beth and Luke exchanged grins when he'd returned to the living room. "He's incorrigible," Luke said. "He always gives them money for their birthdays. I figure it's because he hasn't got enough imagination to buy them suitable gifts."

"I heard that!" Matt called out.

Beth laughed. She was enjoying the friendly banter and all the chaos of Luke's family. This was how a family should be, she thought. Full of fun and love and noise. A tiny pain dug at her in the region of her heart. She'd never had a family like this…and probably never would. Instead, there'd just be Sarah and her. She made a silent vow that Sarah's life would be filled with as much love as this family possessed—if not as much noise.

The back door banged and Sasha came inside, closely followed by Daisy, bringing with her the chill of the snow-covered ground. Matt reappeared in the kitchen doorway, his attention half on what Celeste was up to in the living room and half on what was going on in the kitchen.

Daisy glared at her uncle as though it was somehow his fault that it wasn't her birthday and therefore she wasn't getting any money. Matt pulled out his wallet and withdrew two crisp new ten-dollar bills. "Happy unbirthday, Daisy," he said and handed her one. Her face lit up and she dashed into the living room. "Thanks, Uncle Matt!"

Luke shook his head. "You're pathetic," he said with a smile, then turned to stir a pot of soup on the stove.

Matt went back to supervise the cuddling of Sarah. Beth moved to gaze out at the mountains.

"My brother's stuck on you," Luke said.

Beth glanced back at him, trying to control the flush of pleasure she felt creeping up her face.

Luke folded his arms across his chest and leaned against the kitchen counter again. "The question is, what d'you think of him?"

"W-well, I hardly know him. I haven't really formed an opinion."

"Hogwash!" Luke snorted. "I saw the way you were looking at him just now."

Beth started to deny what he thought he'd seen in her eyes but Luke held up his hand. He fixed her with a glare. "I don't want you breaking his heart. He's a good man. He paid your hospital bill so you wouldn't be facing charges."

Beth felt the breath whoosh from her lungs. "H-he *what?*"

"He didn't tell you?"

Beth could only shake her head. Matt had paid her hospital bill? *All* of it? She felt sick to her stomach that her dishonesty had led to this.

"I have no idea why you lit outta there without paying your bill and without letting anyone know where you were going, Beth, but if you've got some kind of problem, I suggest you share it with the rest of the family. We'll see if we can't find a solution to it. Together."

Although she was initially taken aback by his harsh tone, Beth knew Luke had Matt's best interests at heart. If only her problems were that easy to solve.

Stunned by Luke's revelation about Matt's paying her hospital bill, she was saved from having to respond by more excited squealing from the living room.

"I think everyone else has arrived by the sound of it," Luke said and escorted her out of the kitchen.

The scene that greeted her was nothing short of pandemonium. The room seemed full of adults and children laughing and greeting one another and pushing forward to take a look at Sarah. She recognized Becky and waved to her over the noise and children.

Becky stepped nimbly toward her, carrying a baby on her hip. She kissed Beth on the cheek, her green eyes alight with speculation. "I didn't expect to see you here!" she cried. "So Matt found you, after all."

Before Beth could answer, the baby held out a chubby hand to Beth and gave her a toothy smile. Beth was captivated, envisioning Sarah at this age. "This is Lily, I assume? She's gorgeous!"

"Thank you. Fortunately, she takes after me," Becky said as she caught hold of a slightly less muscular version of Matt and drew him over. "Beth, I'd like you to meet my husband, Will."

Will shook her hand warmly and said, "I'm the thorn in Matt's side." He spoke with total candor. "And I'm delighted to meet you at last, Beth." Deep dimples creased his cheeks and his eyes glittered as he gestured a young boy toward him. "This is our son, Nick."

Beth noticed that the boy walked with a little difficulty but he had a lovely smile and vibrant blue eyes. "Pleased to meet you, Beth," he said, shaking her hand. "Have you met my uncle Jack?"

As he made the introductions, Beth surmised that the boy possessed an intelligence and maturity far beyond his years. Jack seemed the least outgoing of the brothers, a bit standoffish even. Beth didn't have time to contemplate him further when Will turned his attention toward Sarah and asked Celeste, who was repelling all attempts by her sisters to snatch Sarah from her arms, "And who is this living doll?"

Celeste dimpled and Beth could see the family resemblance between uncle and niece. "This is Sarah," she said in a hushed voice, then more loudly, "She's Uncle Matt's new baby."

A deafening silence descended on the room. Beth wished the floor would open up and swallow her. Before she could speak, Matt was beside her.

"I think she's a little confused," he said, then addressed Celeste. "Honey, I wish Sarah was my baby, but I only helped get her mom to the hospital." Matt glanced at Beth, his eyes begging her forgiveness for Celeste's remark.

Beth's heart squeezed with emotion and gratitude. He'd said he wished Sarah was his child! What a wonderful man. What a wonderful father he would've been, if he'd been given the chance.

And then you never would've met him, she thought. *You wouldn't have had the chance to fall in love with him.*

Feeling lightheaded, she sat down on the nearest chair. *Love?* Was that possible? *No!* She tried to deny that what she felt for Matt was love. She'd promised herself she was never going to fall in love again. She'd never leave herself so vulnerable again.

"Beth? Are you okay? Can I get you something?" She looked into Matt's warm brown eyes as he hunkered down in front of her.

She shook her head. "No, I'm fine. I guess I'm not feeling as strong as I thought I was."

The adult occupants of the room watched the exchange in silence. Then, as though embarrassed to have been caught staring, everyone seemed suddenly galvanized into activity. Becky barked orders at the men, handed Lily to Matt and strode into the kitchen. Matt fussed over the children, trying to placate them about whose turn it was to hold which baby. Luke, Will and Jack disappeared out the front door and returned moments later, loaded down with food that they carried through to the kitchen.

Beth stared helplessly at Matt, unable to come up with a thing to say. Finally her tongue came unglued and she said, "I guess they're having a party for Sasha. I should be going."

Matt looked at her curiously. "You're invited, too. Why would you think my family wouldn't want to include you?"

Flustered, Beth cursed her limited and lonely upbringing. She'd never been invited to a big family gathering, never been a part of a big family get-together. Yet for Matt, family events were such a common occurrence that it was perfectly natural to be included. Matt had everything she'd ever wanted—a big, close and happy family. And she'd never be able to provide that for Sarah. She turned away from him to hide her tears.

"Beth?"

"Is there somewhere I can freshen up?" she asked without looking at him.

Matt hesitated as though unsure of what to do next. That only made her heart break more.

He gripped her elbow gently, led her down the hallway and opened a door. "We can go, if you'd rather not stay. I'll understand if they're all too much for you."

Beth met his eyes. His face was so full of concern, she was tempted to stroke his cheek to reassure him. "I'm fine. And I'd love to stay. I'm sure Sarah would, too. She seems to be enjoying all the attention." She indicated the scene at the other end of the hallway, where Daisy was blowing bubbles against Sarah's outstretched hand.

The tension eased from his face and he grinned and threw his arms around her. "I'm glad," he said softly, then bent to kiss her.

At the first touch of his lips, heat infused her. Matt's lips worked their magic and sent desire racing through her. This was madness! Matt's family was less than twenty feet away, and here they were behaving like teenagers. She pushed away from him, glanced down the hallway to make sure no one was watching and forced her voice to sound normal. "Could you give me a moment to freshen up?"

Matt seemed about to say something, then apparently thought better of it. Giving her a tiny salute, he went back to the living room.

Beth closed the bathroom door behind her and leaned against it while she caught her breath. She looked at herself in the mirror and was shocked by her appearance. Her cheeks were flushed, her eyes bright with sensual awareness. She turned on the faucet and splashed cold water over her face. What was wrong with her? She had no business falling in love with Matt O'Malley!

No! She *wasn't* in love with him. It was simply seeing

him here with his family, seeing the love they had for him and for each other, that had her thinking along those lines.

AFTER THE BIRTHDAY LUNCH had concluded, they drove off to the laughter of the children as they threw snowballs in the yard.

When they got to the intersection where the road joined the highway that went toward Pine Ridge, Matt pulled over, rested his left arm on the steering wheel and turned toward her.

"Are you up to seeing the surprise I told you about or would you prefer to go home?"

Beth wanted to go home where she planned to ask Matt why he'd paid her hospital bill. But the look of anticipation in his eyes had meant her deciding that their conversation could wait. "I love surprises. Lead on."

He rewarded her with a smile and got back onto the road. They eventually turned off it into another valley and drove along a river for several miles until finally Matt headed toward the foothills. He stopped his truck on the empty road.

"What do you think?" he asked, a note of pride in his voice.

Beth gazed out at the rolling snow-covered countryside set against the foothills. "It's beautiful," she said. "Like one of those Christmas cards with the pine forests and Santa's sleigh sliding across the snow."

Matt drove farther toward the hills and pulled up in a clearing of lodgepole pine. "We're here," he said and climbed out. He came to open her door and took her hand to help her down from his truck. When she had her feet planted firmly in the snow, he said, "This is where I'm going to build my family home."

Chapter Thirteen

Taken aback, Beth turned in a full circle, absorbing the scenery that stretched in all directions. She put her hand over her heart and said, "It's breathtaking."

Matt gazed down at her, his expression pensive. "I'm glad you think so."

"It's so beautiful. It must've cost you a great deal of money." Then realizing how mercenary that sounded, Beth said, "I'm sorry, that was a dreadful thing to say. It's just that I'm well aware of the price of real estate around here, and I imagine something like this would be astronomically expensive."

Matt grinned. "I got it at a discount. Will owned two hundred acres and subdivided it into ranchettes in order to save the historical part of Spruce Lake."

Beth stared at him. "Will did that?"

"He did a lot more. Not all of it good." Matt threw her a crooked smile. "One of these days, I'll tell you the whole story."

Sarah let out a protesting squawk and Matt scooped her out of her carrier, lifted her into the sling he wore beneath his jacket and fastened her into it. When he pulled his jacket protectively around her, she settled immediately.

Beth watched his actions with her daughter and thought,

This is exactly the kind of man I'd want as a father for my children.

Before Matt could detect the longing that must be written all over her face, she glanced around and said, "I'm afraid I've lost my bearings. Where's the ranch from here?"

"A couple of valleys over." He inclined his head, then reached for her hand and they continued walking deeper into the clearing. There were poles sticking out of the snow with red tape attached to them. He walked to the center of the marked-out area and said, "This is where I'm planning to build come spring."

The view here was spellbinding. Across the valley, the forested hillsides rose up to snow-covered peaks. In summer, the fields would be covered in green, the spruce and pines forming a dark band above. And where the forests thinned out, high in the mountains, a little of the snow would still remain, slowly melting until the fall. The aspens would provide fiery bursts of yellow, orange and red as their leaves changed. Beth knew all this because she'd seen it happen from the sanctuary of her cabin. But Matt's view was far superior to the one she had on Blue Spruce Drive.

A creek ran below the home site, its surface covered with ice that had melted in places. She could hear water trickling beneath and pictured it as a rushing stream during summer, kids fishing for trout or playing in the shallows. "I've run out of superlatives," she said with a shrug. "I couldn't imagine a more idyllic setting for a home."

She gestured at the area within the poles. "This is a large home for one person."

Matt looked away to the valley for a moment, as though collecting his thoughts. "I figured it's time I started planning for the future...."

Beth appreciated what it must've taken Matt to admit

that. One's life didn't end with the death of a spouse; it just went on hold while the grieving process ran its course. Some courses took longer than others. Matt was young and virile. He had a lot to offer some lucky woman. It was right that he should move on from his grief and start planning for the future.

Pain twisted in her heart. What would she do without Matt in her life? In Sarah's? She glanced out to the view of the valley. *If only I could put the past few months behind me and start planning something concrete for the rest of my life. Setting solid foundations to ensure Sarah's happiness.*

She drew in a deep breath. It all seemed so hard, too much to do alone. Expelling her breath, she turned back to Matt. "Tell me where everything's going to be."

He grinned as if happy that she cared. And she did. More than she wanted to. Because one day soon, she had to leave Matt and take positive steps toward the next stage of her life.

"We're standing in the living room. There'll be a fireplace against that wall," he explained with a sweep of his hand. "The entry's here and over there is the dining room."

He strode through his imaginary house, pointing out each area. "Study here, kitchen, family room. The stairs to the children's bedrooms will be there—" he hesitated, took a breath, then continued "—and the master suite is at the end on this level."

He stopped in the area marked out for the master suite. "It looks out on both the valley view and the forest and mountains. There'll be a fireplace in here, as well."

Beth smiled up at him. "I like the master suite being on the first floor. You've obviously put real thought into this."

"I have," he said and smiled. "Will and Becky own the lot next door. I'd like to start building in late spring, just as soon as I've worked out how I want the exterior to look."

"I'm an architect. I can visualize what a home in such a location could look like. Do you want some advice?"

Matt cupped her cheek. "I'd like that very much."

Matt wasn't wearing gloves, yet his hand was warm against her cold cheek. She wanted to remember and savor the sensation.

She cleared her throat. "You mentioned children's bedrooms. How many?" She'd experienced a strange sense of protectiveness when he'd talked about the children's rooms—as though *she* wanted to be the mother of those children.

"Kids? Or bedrooms?"

"I meant how many bedrooms did you plan for upstairs. But I suppose it would be better to start with how many children you eventually see yourself needing to house."

RIGHT NOW, HE DIDN'T have any. Maybe he never would. Suddenly Matt felt foolish for bringing her here. He was thirty-five; his child-rearing years were probably behind him.

"Matt?" Beth's soft inquiry brought him back from a dark place he didn't want to visit. He couldn't imagine his life without kids. His own kids.

He shrugged. "I always wanted a big family. How about you?"

She smiled, her eyes dreamy. "I hadn't thought beyond Sarah. But a big family would be nice." She reached out to stroke Sarah's back through his jacket. "I like being a mom and that, I can assure you, *is* the truth!"

Matt urged her into his arms, careful not to crush Sarah sleeping in the sling between them. "That's nice.

I like a woman who enjoys motherhood." He slipped his hands inside her jacket, needing to touch her. Needing her warmth.

"Sarah and I had a pretty shaky start, mostly due to my ineptitude, but I love her so much. More than I ever thought possible."

"Must be a good feeling."

"But you love your nieces and nephew."

"Yeah, I do. Unreservedly. But I don't have to live with them day in and day out, or make decisions for them that could possibly affect their whole lives. I don't have that sort of responsibility. But I'd welcome it if it came along."

"Your attitude is a refreshing change." Beth stood on tiptoe and kissed the end of his nose, then stepped back, as though startled by her impulsiveness.

Matt smiled slowly. "You can do that again if you want."

"Do it again? I'm not even sure why I did it in the first place!" She laughed and spun away from him.

Matt watched her for a few minutes, delighted by the blush creeping up her cheeks. "Okay, Ms. Big City Architect, how do *you* see my home?" he asked, to break the tension.

Beth walked out his imaginary front door and turned to look at his proposed house. "Chinked log slabs cladding the outside and stone—a warm ochre with dried moss on it—would suit these surroundings perfectly. And inside, the same stone, cladding a full-height fireplace. The dining room should have a wall of windows that open to the view."

Matt nodded. "Go on."

"I love the idea of the children's rooms upstairs. The ones at the rear would have the most adorable view into the trees. I expect a bunny or deer to pop out of the forest at any moment. It's absolutely enchanting. But I'd like to suggest the kitchen be at the rear rather than the front of the house."

Matt's heart sank. "I like the view, though."

"You can still have the view, only make the family room here at the front, and then the kitchen can take advantage of both the view to the rear, where children can play under supervision, and your valley vista, which will be visible through the family room. Put an island workstation here. A big farmhouse table there, so the kids can do their homework near Mom or take their meals. The sinks could go here," she said, walking through the "rooms," gesturing with her hands, "so the view's into the trees. Cooktop there, oven, fridge and a large countertop where they won't disrupt your views of the valley and the mountains beyond."

"That's what my plans lacked, a woman's touch. An expert's opinion on how to maximize what I've got. I love it all. Please continue," he said, reaching inside his jacket to rub Sarah's back.

She pointed out where the laundry and mudroom should be, as well as a powder room. "Now—" she said, retracing her steps to the master suite "—there's so much potential here to create something outstanding."

Matt loved hearing the passion in her voice as she described what she envisioned for his home and outlined plans that, until now, had been vague scratchings in a sketchbook.

"I think this room should have a pitched ceiling and plenty of glass to take in your views of both the forest and the valley. Master bath over here, walk-in closets there and a cozy sitting area. You could even put a small nursery off the sitting area."

"That sounds like an awful lot to fit into one house."

"Not really. The floor area you've marked out is substantial and it befits a home in this kind of location. Most people don't realize how big a house ends up being. I've had clients complain about how small their foundation looks, but when the house is completed, they're pleasantly surprised."

Matt rubbed his chin. "I'd better commission you for a more accurate plan and drawings. What do you charge for your services?"

She swatted his arm. "I wouldn't dream of payment. First, because I couldn't possibly repay you for everything you've done for Sarah and me, and second, because you're my friend." She paused, her head cocked to the side. "Or at least I hope you are."

Matt pulled her to him and wrapped his arms loosely around her. "Let me leave you in no doubt as to that assumption," he said and kissed her.

BETH WAS SWEPT AWAY on a wave of tenderness as Matt's lips covered hers. She had to hang on to his shoulders to combat the dazzling effect of being kissed so thoroughly, so tenderly. He teased her with tiny kisses along her bottom lip, then increased the intensity, encouraging her to follow suit while he drew her close, sending fingers of warmth licking through her.

She wanted to get even closer, but Sarah was between them and starting to squirm.

Matt moved back, still gazing into her eyes. "Wow," he said softly.

At a loss for words, she smiled.

Then he said, "I wish I could keep you smiling like that for the rest of my life."

Beth wanted to ask what he meant by that, but Sarah was fussing, his soothing strokes failing for once to settle her. "I think she's hungry," she managed to say and then cleared her throat. "We won't make it home in time. I'd better feed her in the truck."

They returned to his vehicle and Matt helped her in, lifted Sarah from her sling and handed her to Beth.

The engine was running, so the cab was warm. Too warm. She left the door open, unzipped her jacket, raised her T-shirt and held Sarah to her breast. Matt turned away and started back toward his home site.

"Where are you going?"

He turned back and said, "To give you some privacy."

"Stay. Please?" Beth extended her hand. "We like having you near us."

MATT SWALLOWED AGAINST the emotions welling in his throat and climbed into the driver's side. Beth's attention had returned to Sarah as she nursed contentedly.

His mouth went dry at the sight he was sure he'd never tire of. She glanced at him and smiled, and the most intense pain gripped his chest. *This is love,* he thought as he gazed back at her. *This is what it feels like to need someone, to truly want her—heart and mind, body and soul.*

He'd been deeply in love with Sally. They were childhood sweethearts who'd been together so long they knew every nuance of each other's thoughts. But the love he felt for Beth was different, and he couldn't figure out why.

The moon, now visible during the daytime, flirted with him through the window. He wanted everything he'd denied himself for so long—companionship, commitment, intimacy...*love.* He wanted to share Beth's bed every night and wake up with her in his arms every morning.

He looked down at sweet little Sarah, already so precious to him. He wanted to be there to watch her grow and utter her first words. He wanted to teach her to ride her first bike, take her to her first day at school, watch with pride as his beautiful daughter headed off to the senior prom.

Sarah would be his daughter. He and Beth could have more children—brothers and sisters for Sarah.... They could be a happy family...live in his home, safe in his love.

"Don't," he heard her whisper and glanced up. Her face was stricken. "Don't start thinking about things that can't be, Matt."

She'd read him so easily. "How'd you know what I was thinking?"

"Because I've been thinking the same things," she admitted candidly. She smiled but her eyes were sad. "The past few days, I've dreamed about how wonderful it would be to share my life with someone like you."

Matt's spirits rose. Was there a chance for them? Then she dashed his hopes like a wave crashing on a rocky shore. "You're a genuinely kind person, Matt. You're so good with Sarah. You *care* about people. That's part of what makes you a great lawman. But we haven't got a future together."

He forced his next words through lips numb with pain. "Why do you believe that?"

She held up her hand. "Don't ask me why. Please."

He let it rest for the moment. There wasn't any point in pressing her. He had to bide his time, convince her with patience and love that they did have a future together. He made a silent vow. *I'll protect you with my life. Both of you.*

"What's the matter?" she asked. "You look so solemn."

"I'm falling in love with you."

"Oh, Matt," she breathed.

"I realize it's probably too soon for you. I don't expect

you to feel the same way...." He caught her hand. "I want to marry you. I want us to be a family." There! He'd said it. He sat back and waited for her reaction.

When she continued to stare at him as if stunned beyond speech, he said, "I've scared you, haven't I?"

"No...I'm just a little bowled over by...what you said."

He wasn't usually impulsive. In fact, he was regarded by the family as the least impulsive of all the O'Malleys, yet his feelings for Beth had stirred him to make a rash declaration. If Will only knew, he'd be snorting with glee.

Dreading her answer, in case she thought he was a witless fool for admitting he loved her when they'd met barely a week ago, he nevertheless needed to know. "Good surprise or bad?"

She smiled, and the radiance of it warmed him to his toes. "Nice surprise."

Matt released his breath, hoping she'd say more. She took her time, as if considering her words.

"A *very* nice surprise," she said.

Feeling he needed to explain himself, he said, "Something happened when I met you. Everything in my training, my instincts, told me to be wary of you, but something kept drawing me back. Being around you and Sarah stirred up feelings in me that were long buried. I felt *compelled* to be with you."

She raised her eyebrows in query.

"You're not ready to hear that, are you?"

"Matt...that's so touching. It seems...out of character for you to admit that."

"A lot of things I've been doing lately are out of character for me."

"Such as?"

"Putting my job on the line by protecting a supposed fugitive from the LAPD."

"You don't believe I am anymore. Do you?" she asked and passed Sarah to him.

"No." He got out and fastened Sarah securely into her baby seat. "I always felt there was something suspicious about those reports," he said, then climbed back into the driver's seat.

"And paying my hospital bill?"

Matt stilled. "Luke told you."

"As he should. Matt… I don't know what to say. I intended to pay, when everything was sorted out. I'd thought of paying it in cash with the money from the safety-deposit box, but that would've attracted too much attention. Besides, I already need to pay back a few thousand dollars of that."

She sighed and looked at him, her eyes filled with pain. "Why did you pay my bill?"

"Because it was the right thing to do."

"You didn't even know me!"

"I knew you were afraid of something—and I figured you had a good reason for running away. I thought maybe there was an abusive husband in the picture, but when I did the check on your license and found out about…Marcus, my fears about that were allayed."

"But before that, you knew nothing about me. Yet you paid my bill." She shook her head. "I don't know what to say," she repeated.

"You don't have to say anything. I didn't want you facing charges in Peaks County for skipping out on your hospital bill." He shrugged. "I had the money. It's no big deal."

"It *is* a big deal. And I'll repay you just as soon as I can. I have insurance, but I couldn't use my real name at the hospital."

Matt covered her hand. "I know all that. I'm a cop, remember? I can tell the real criminals from the fake ones, and your story stank worse than last Friday's fish dinner!"

Beth laughed and said, "Thank you for saving me from the clutches of the county law." Then she grew serious. "You're a very special man, Matt O'Malley." She leaned forward and kissed him, then pulled back and looked deep into his eyes. "A *very* special man."

Matt's spirits soared at her compliment.

"Let's go home," she said in a way that had Matt wanting that more than anything.

"All set?" he asked, his voice husky.

"Just a moment." Beth put her hand over his as he reached for the ignition. "I want to have one last look before we leave."

BETH GAZED BACK at where Matt planned to build his home. When she'd arrived here an hour ago, she'd been captivated by its beauty. Knowing this was where he wanted to raise his family, she felt a sense of yearning and sorrow.

She'd love more than anything to be Matt's wife, but knew that could never be. In spite of his declaration that he'd protect her, she and Sarah would never be safe as long as Hennessey and Morgan were free. And in spite of what he thought, neither would Matt. As soon as she was well enough, she had to leave Spruce Lake, to protect them all.

Chapter Fourteen

When Matt returned to the living room after getting Sarah settled in her room, Beth was sitting cross-legged on the sofa, drawing on an art tablet. She covered her drawing when he leaned over to take a look.

"Uh-uh. No peeking," she said. "Go fix us a snack and by the time you get back, I might have some sketches worth looking at."

He fixed mugs of hot chocolate and grilled cheese sandwiches, then took them to the living room, set them on the coffee table and stood watching Beth as she worked.

Her silky blond hair fell forward as she bent over the sketch pad, intent on her task. He longed to reach out and tangle his fingers in the golden tresses but tried to ignore that desire. Instead, he watched, fascinated, as her hands flew over the page, sketching, shading, scribbling, oblivious to his presence. Finally he cleared his throat.

Beth glanced up and patted the sofa beside her. "Come see what I've done so far."

He handed her the hot chocolate and sat down beside her. "Mmm, that's perfect," she said after taking a sip, then gave him one of her radiant smiles.

Encouraged, Matt moved closer and looked down at the sketch pad.

The handsome residence was everything he'd ever

wanted in a home and a whole lot more. When Beth had gone through the imaginary rooms back at his land and made vague motions describing how the exterior should look, he'd done his best to understand the concepts she was outlining. But here was the salient proof of her vision.

He shook his head in wonder. "It's perfect. Absolutely perfect."

"They're only rough sketches," she pointed out.

"It doesn't matter. I'm impressed by your talent. You've captured everything I wanted in my home, but you've made it...so much more." He indicated parts of the sketch. "It's got that cozy mountain-home look to it—like it's somewhere you'd always feel welcome, always find shelter. But then you've added these architectural elements...." He shrugged. "They've lifted it above the ordinary and given it an individual flair, a personality. It's remarkable."

"Then I assume I have a happy client?"

He clasped her chin and brought her mouth to his, kissing her gently. Sensing her hesitation, he drew away. Something was bothering her, but he didn't want to confront it right now. Didn't want to spoil the mood.

"I'm glad you like it," she said and turned the page. "Now, how about we haggle over the floor plans?"

During the short time he'd been in the kitchen, she'd sketched the outline of floor plans, too. Beth took a bite of the sandwich, murmured her appreciation, then picked up her pencil and started sketching in more detail. "This is very rough, you understand. I'd need to run a tape over the areas you've got marked out, but I think it's reasonably accurate."

"It's perfect," he said again. "Thank you."

BETH EXPERIENCED a tingling sensation at Matt's closeness and yearned for more. The here and now was what she would make the most of—taking every moment with Matt and making it special—because soon she'd have to leave. To keep them all safe.

"I'll do concept drawings of each room so you and your contractors have a clear understanding of what the finished product should look like. And I'll do detailed drawings of certain architectural elements." She studied Matt. His mouth was mere inches from her eyes. She admired the texture of his lips and ached to have him kiss her again.

She'd been startled by the kiss last night. Until then she hadn't realized that Matt was attracted to her. And then out of left field had come that sudden admission that he was falling in love with her. She'd been churlish not to respond in kind, but Beth didn't know what to say.

To take his declaration seriously, to get involved with Matt, filled her with a longing that reached deep inside her. But Beth couldn't risk exploring it. She and Sarah would have to go. The net Hennessey had cast was closing around her. Leaving Matt would tear her apart.

"Sweetheart?"

"Mmm?" Beth blinked back her tears.

"A penny for them," he said, his voice so warm and tender.

She placed her hands on either side of his strong jaw and drew his face toward hers. If only she could find a solution that would really keep her and Sarah safe. She closed her eyes. When she opened them again, Matt was smiling. "Kiss me," he said.

Beth complied, putting everything she felt for him into it—her passion, her gratitude, her unspoken love. She pressed her lips to his. Once, twice, three times. Then she slipped the tip of her tongue between his lips.

MATT COULD STAND the teasing no longer. To hell with control and being noble. He lifted her onto his lap so she straddled him, his hands cupping her bottom.

"I want to make love to you," he murmured against her mouth, then nipped gently at her bottom lip. "I want it so badly."

"Me, too," she admitted, surprising him with her response.

"But I know it's too soon. When do you think we can?"

A loud cry from the nursery had them both instantly alert.

"Great timing," he muttered and went to get up, but Beth pressed a hand to his chest and climbed off his lap. "No. I'll go."

Matt watched her leave the room. Everything tingled, including his calluses. He needed to take another trip to the woodpile. Although it was in danger of getting so big it would soon be higher than the cabin, he stood and staggered outside.

WHEN MATT CAME BACK inside a half hour later, he washed up at the sink, dried his hands and started to apply Lucy's salve. The ointment was working wonders, but he wished he could give splitting wood a rest.

Beth appeared in the kitchen. "Sarah's down for a few hours," she said, then took the tube from him. "Let me do that. It's about time I looked after you for a change." She smoothed the salve over his palms and reached into a drawer for two bandages. She began to wrap his hands. "Maybe these will remind you that you shouldn't be splitting any more wood," she said and smiled mischievously up at him.

"Should I fix us something to eat?" he suggested,

needing to do something with his hands other than pulling Beth into his arms. He'd gone way too far on the sofa. Until Beth was recovered enough to make love, he needed to slow down.

"We just had grilled cheese sandwiches a little while ago!"

"I'm hungry already. I defrosted steaks this morning. Can't let them go to waste."

"I make a mean mushroom sauce," Beth said.

Matt took her hand as she turned away. He dropped a kiss on her palm. "You didn't answer my question earlier," he reminded her. "When can we make love?"

She swallowed at the intimacy of his words. "Four or five weeks," she said. "I'm sorry."

Matt hauled her into his arms. She looked so vulnerable, so disappointed. He kissed the end of her nose. "Don't be. The waiting will make it all the more worthwhile."

BETH'S LEGS NEARLY buckled under her at the sexual tension in his words, in the room. If only they *had* a few weeks...

Matt prepared the griddle and laid two big steaks on it, then bent to kiss the delicate skin beneath her ear. "You're quiet," he said. "What's up?"

Unable to look at him, she dumped the sliced mushrooms into a pan with melted butter and stirred.

Matt took the spoon out of her hand, put it on the counter and turned toward her. "Something's troubling you. What is it?"

Beth shrugged. There was no way she was going to confront the fact that she was leaving as soon as she could get away from the cabin. From Matt.

Unfortunately, he mistook her shrug and said, "I know we can't make love yet. But in a few weeks, I'll be able to show you how I really feel. No holds barred." He clasped her hips and tugged her toward him. "I just wanted to warn you about that."

Beth was afraid to wonder what exactly Matt could mean by "no holds barred." If only she could be here in a few weeks' time to find out. She placed a hand on his chest and managed to say, "I can't wait." Guilt overwhelmed her. How many more lies would she tell him?

She returned to the pan that had been forgotten on the stove, picked up the spoon and scraped the bottom. Then she crumbled a stock cube, stirred it through and added cream.

"That smells delicious," he said.

"As soon as you get the salad made we can eat," she murmured, trying to distract him from talking about their future. "The steaks look about done."

She turned off the burner and put a lid on the pan to keep the mushroom sauce warm, and set the table. Matt lit some candles, then pulled out her chair. She touched her juice glass to his bottle of beer. "What will we toast?"

"Everlasting happiness? Love? A fantastic sex life?"

Beth giggled. "Stop that!"

"What can I say? You bring out the playful side in me."

"Don't you get tired of having to be responsible all the time?"

"No. Never. It's always come easily to me. It's not something I consciously do or think about. Why do you ask?"

"I thought you'd welcome a break from it occasionally. Yet here you are, taking time off, being responsible for Sarah and me."

He covered her hand. "What I welcome is the responsibility. I love you both, so it's not a chore."

WHEN THEY FINISHED their salads, Matt got up to serve the steak. He set Beth's plate on the table in front of her, together with the jug of sauce. Her eyes widened. "I can't eat all that!" She carved off a tiny section of the steak, then forked the rest onto his plate.

"You'll have to cultivate a heartier appetite than that if you're going to fit in at the ranch," he said. "We raise beef cattle. Mighty fine ones."

Beth forced herself to laugh. There he was again, talking about their future together as though it was a dead certainty. She said, "I love steak as much as the next person, but I don't have the stomach for so much food."

"Well, I do." Matt poured the mushroom sauce over his generous serving, then cut into it, sighing around the first mouthful. "The mushroom sauce is fantastic."

"Thank you. I'm not much of a cook, so over the years, I've perfected a number of sauces to disguise the taste of anything I've messed up."

Matt swallowed his mouthful and grinned. "Becky's not much of a cook, either. However, she hasn't perfected anything to cover the fact. Will does all the cooking in their house."

"Smart woman for marrying him."

Matt took a mouthful of beer, then put his bottle back on the table, twirling it between his fingers. "Not without a lot of persuading on his part."

Beth smiled. Talking about Matt's family helped alleviate some of the tension she was feeling. "I like people who don't give up."

"Will's very determined when he wants something. He was the bane of my existence until Becky took over as his keeper. We're complete opposites, yet look the most alike."

"What happened to Luke's wife?"

"Tory ran out on him just after Celeste was born. She specialized in tying Luke up in knots by running away from home on a whim. The last time was with a rodeo champion."

"Oh, my! Poor Luke and his little girls."

Matt grimaced. "She wasn't mentally stable. Luke suffered terribly during their marriage, but he tried to make it work."

"I'm sorry.…"

"Then there's Jack. He was studying for the priesthood, but he left the seminary and came back to town a couple of years ago."

"Why did he leave?"

"Don't know. He's never opened up about it and none of us will push him. He's making a good living as a contractor and master carpenter. He'll be building my house."

He stretched out his legs and said, "Adam's the youngest. He's a firefighter in Boulder."

"Why not here?"

"He doesn't like small-town life. Though I'm not sure Boulder really qualifies as the big city. You'll get to meet him one of these days."

Since Beth wouldn't be anywhere in the vicinity of Spruce Lake for much longer, that was unlikely. She tried to comfort herself with the thought that once she left town, Matt could get on with his life and forget about her. He was ready to think about remarrying. Beth assumed there'd been no shortage of women in his life after Sally's death.

"Have you dated many women since your wife passed away?" she asked.

Matt looked at her, obviously bewildered. "No. I haven't been interested in dating anyone."

His blunt admission had her wondering. How could any woman possibly live up to his memories of Sally?

Beth figured she must be some sort of masochist when she couldn't stop herself from asking, "Why not?"

Matt got up from the table and took their empty plates to the sink. He turned back to her and leaned against the counter, bracing his hands on either side of him. His knuckles were white.

"I've found relationships very difficult since Sally died. I've been consumed by guilt, knowing that had I not been so diligent about my job, I might've been able to save Sally and the baby. Every time I thought of them, my gut burned with guilt. But being with you and Sarah…has made me confront my past and realize I can finally move on."

He took a deep breath and said, "These past few years… I've felt unworthy of being loved, even by my family."

His pain was palpable. Beth's heart squeezed into a tiny knot of self-loathing. It had taken Matt so long to allow himself to love again and now she was going to hurt him by leaving. "I'm sorry you felt this way," she whispered.

He reached out to clasp her hand, drawing her to him. Beth stood and put her arms around him and held him close. "You're a good man, Matt. You deserve every happiness in life."

"Thank you," he said, and turned to fill the sink with water.

Unable to bear the pain in those two simple words, Beth wrapped her arms around him from behind and rested her head against his back, breathing in his warmth, his strength.

"I've always been called solid, dependable, sensible. I've never been the life of the party and I've hardly ever done an impulsive thing in my life. In a nutshell, I'm boring," he said, astounding her.

"What?" She turned him to face her. "I don't think you're the least bit boring. The fact that you came searching

for me was very impulsive. And heroic. You're solid, dependable and sensible, and there isn't anything wrong with that." She cradled his face in her hands and forced him to look into her eyes. "There's nothing I'd want to change about you. Those are qualities to be cherished in a man. And I cherish them very dearly. Matt?"

"Yes?"

"Kiss me," she said, and ran her hands up beneath his T-shirt.

Matt's body responded to her soft touch, the scratch of her fingernails. "You're heading into dangerous territory," he whispered hoarsely.

She blinked coquettishly and said, "Oh?" but continued her onslaught, her nails marching up his chest.

"Don't do this to me." He groaned. "A man can only take so much." He placed his hands over hers to still them. "You're gonna have to stop that right now," he growled. "This is sheer torture...."

Beth kissed him, then stepped back. "But you feel *so* good," she purred.

"You're stealing my lines," he protested, and gnawed lightly on her lip.

"Oh, Matt," she sighed. "If only..."

Matt quirked his eyebrow and grinned. "Yeah, if only," he said, gazing at her with open affection.

"Let's make out," she whispered against his mouth.

HE SWALLOWED THE LUMP that had lodged firmly in his throat. What was she suggesting?

Beth clasped both his hands. "Remember back in high school when you used to fool around? Remember how good it felt? How naughty but exciting?"

Not for the first time, Matt's mouth went dry. "Uh-huh."

She leaned toward him and whispered in his ear, her

warm breath on his cheek, sending delicious prickles of sensation to where he didn't need them right now. "Let's fool around."

The hairs on the back of his neck stood at attention, but he made himself shake his head emphatically. *No.* As he'd said, there was only so much he could take.

Beth ran a finger down his cheek. "Come on. It'll be fun," she urged, leaning even closer.

Matt gripped her arms. He thought he'd pass out if he didn't.

"Come on," she murmured. "Let's go into the living room and pretend we're at the movies. We'll neck and get all hot and bothered."

Matt groaned.

"Don't you want to?" she asked softly.

"You know I do. But we're not kids anymore. I don't want to end up embarrassing myself. And believe me, I know I will. Probably long before we even get near the sofa."

Beth smiled mischievously. She seemed determined to push him to his limits. As it was, her sexy talk had him at the point of exploding.

She was a temptress, no doubt about it.

Chapter Fifteen

Los Angeles

Hennessey cursed when he saw the computer screen. "I go away for the weekend and that's when the damned woman rears her head," he shouted, thumping the desk. "Morgan!" he yelled. "Get in here!"

"What's up?" Morgan sauntered into the office and sprawled in the only other chair the office contained.

Hennessey swung the computer screen around so he could read the details. "What the *hell* have you been up to while I was away?" he demanded.

Morgan looked at the screen and whistled softly. "Colorado? We've been searching for her all over California and she's in *Colorado?* Who does she know there that'd hide her this long? That check I did on her friends was so thorough it included people she was friends with back in elementary school. *Nobody* lives in Colorado."

Hennessey chose to ignore the fact that Morgan hadn't caught the information glaring at him from the computer screen. If he'd been this lax in keeping track of any references to Elizabeth Whitman-Wyatt coming through their police computer systems, Hennessey doubted he'd been as thorough as he claimed about the background checks. Someone from the Sheriff's Department in Spruce Lake,

Colorado, had accessed information about her driver's license. He needed to get out there, and soon.

With a snort of disgust, he turned back to the screen. Morgan would pay for his mistake once they found her. "Locate this Spruce Lake place. Then book us on the next flight out there." He snatched up the phone and put through a call to the sheriff's department in Spruce Lake.

"SORRY, I CAN'T TELL YOU anything else, Detective," Ben Hansen said. "But as I mentioned, Matt O'Malley's the one to speak to. He helped this woman—Beth Whitman-Wyatt? I could've sworn Matt said her surname was something else. She crashed her car the night she had the baby, then checked out of the hospital and disappeared. I know Sheriff O'Malley was looking for her. Why don't I have him give you a call tomorrow? He'll be in the office first thing."

"Don't bother," Hennessey muttered. "You've told me all I need to know." He rang off and turned to Morgan. "Seems that goddamned woman changed her name since she moved to Colorado."

"How can you be sure it's her, then?"

"The undersheriff confirmed she'd recently had a baby." He slapped his thigh. "I *knew* I couldn't trust you to keep on top of this!"

Morgan shrugged. "Hey, you're the one who took off to Mexico for a couple of days."

Hennessey had to force himself not to sucker punch the other man. His reasons for heading to Mexico were none of Morgan's damned business. He had a nice little people-smuggling business going that neither Morgan nor Marcus Jackson were involved in. More than once he'd regretted that the people-smuggling had taken up so much of his time that he'd let Jackson handle the money and drugs from busts they hadn't reported. And the profits from their blackmail book...

The week before his death, Jackson had given him a key to a safety-deposit box, claiming that was where their stuff was stored. Only problem was, when he'd gone to use it, the box was empty.

He'd confronted Jackson, things had turned nasty and a bullet through the kneecaps hadn't convinced Jackson he should hand over the correct key. Unfortunately, his next bullet, which was supposed to glance off the side of Marcus Jackson's ear, had gone straight into his brain.

Hennessey had cursed the gun he'd purchased from a backstreet dealer earlier that day, wiped off his prints and thrown it into a nearby Dumpster. He'd fired several shots from his service revolver into the air to create a cover story, then called in to report that his partner was down. Within minutes the alley in south central L.A. was crawling with cops who'd raced to assist a fellow officer. He told them he'd pursued his partner's killer, fired off several shots, then seen the man throw his weapon into the Dumpster. He'd been too concerned about his fallen buddy, he said, to pursue the culprit farther. The murder weapon was duly found and Hennessey was hailed a hero for risking his life trying to save his partner; he'd even attempted the full CPR routine. He'd actually managed to squeeze out some token tears when interrogated over the incident later that evening.

Furious that he had no idea where the key was hidden or which bank it was for, he'd turned their office upside down searching for it. The only conclusion he could come to was that it had to be at Jackson's house. He'd thought that he'd scared the hell out of Jackson's wife and she'd hand it over. Instead, she'd given him the slip. When he caught up with her, she was going to pay dearly for her treachery.

"So now we fly out to Colorado and deal with her?"

Hennessey's head snapped around to Morgan's. "Yes. Did you book our flight?"

"We're on the 6:00 a.m. to Denver."

"Why not tonight?"

Morgan glanced at his watch. "Because the last flight to Denver is probably taxiing down the runway right now." He looked up with what seemed suspiciously like triumph and said, "Even you don't have the power to stop that."

Hennessey forced himself to put aside the happy prospect of disposing of Morgan; for now he needed the little weasel.

"We'll get into Denver around nine-thirty," Morgan was saying, "and then we have to drive to this godforsaken place. That's another two hours. Tomorrow's soon enough to catch up with her, get the key and get rid of her and the kid."

Hennessey's lip curled with pleasure. "I'm looking forward to seeing that little bitch again...."

BETH WAS IN THE CABIN'S kitchen, gazing out into the moonlight, contemplating how to tell Matt she was leaving, when she became aware of his presence.

She turned toward him. Matt smiled slowly and crossed his arms in a gesture she'd come to love. He was dressed only in jeans, his chest bare. He looked magnificent standing there, all rippling muscles, five-o'clock shadow—and masculine need. Marcus had never wanted her that much.

He raked a hand through his hair. "You drive me crazy. Keep looking at me like that and I don't know how we're going to wait...."

His need for her found a similar response in Beth, because she wanted him every bit as much as he so obviously wanted her.

She touched his cheek. "You know all the right things to say."

Matt crossed his arms again, as though needing to do something with them other than hold her. She considered asking him what he was thinking, but was afraid of the answer.

She poured two mugs of hot chocolate, then gave one to him. "Let's take these into the living room."

"So we can pretend we're at the movies and fool around some more?" he teased as he followed her in.

Beth covered her face with her free hand. "I'm so embarrassed I said that! It's not like me to be so bold."

Matt leaned toward her and kissed the end of her nose. "I loved it. Every teasing, exciting, wonderful moment of it. Do it again sometime. Anytime."

A DEEP SENSE OF contentment filled him. Would this passion they shared last long into their marriage, the way it had for his parents? He hoped so. He had to believe it would, but in order to do that, he had to believe there *was* a future for him and Beth.

However, any chance of having a future together meant he needed to have the corrupt cops in L.A. brought to justice. *And* he had to do it behind Beth's back; if she got wind of what he was up to, she'd take off in a second. The one thing in Beth's favor was that Hennessey didn't know she was being protected by a cop. And Matt was more than willing to protect her—and Sarah—with his life.

His cell rang. He checked to see who the caller was, then cursed softly. "I told Ben not to call me unless it's urgent. Excuse me," he said and went into her bedroom.

A sense of foreboding trickled its unwelcome way

through Beth when he closed her door to take the call. She was ninety-nine percent sure the call was about her. The fact that he'd taken the call behind closed doors virtually confirmed it. Beth *had* to know. Tiptoeing to the bedroom, she put her ear against the door, straining to hear. Matt was being very quiet. What if he'd finished the call and then pulled the door open to find her snooping?

"When was this?" Matt demanded, his tone gruff. "And what did you tell him?"

His next words confirmed her worst fears.

"I wish you hadn't said anything. You should've passed the call to me. In future, if anyone asks, she's left the county."

Beth felt as though the air had been crushed from her lungs. The call he was talking about must have been from Hennessey. He'd tracked her down to the sheriff's office in Spruce Lake and made inquiries! Her legs nearly buckled beneath her.

"It doesn't matter how I know." Matt was clearly losing patience. "I'll be in the office in the morning. If you get any more questions about her, give the caller my number but don't say anything else. Okay?"

Beth spun away from the door and staggered to the sofa, her heart pounding. She had to get out of here! Hennessey had tracked her to Spruce Lake, and if Matt got in the way he'd kill him, just as he'd killed Marcus.

When Matt returned, Beth clasped her hands together in her lap to still their trembling. Forcing herself to breathe as normally as possible, she smiled up at him and asked, "Business?"

He combed his hand through his hair. "I have to go into town tomorrow to sort out some paperwork," he said and sat down, taking her in his arms. "It'll only be a couple of hours. Do you mind?"

Beth shook her head, convinced that Hennessey knew exactly where she was. She had to leave Spruce Lake as soon as possible. If she could get straight on a bus, in two hours she'd be in Denver, or well on her way to Grand Junction.

"I want you and Sarah to come with me," he said.

"No!"

"Excuse me?"

Beth fought to control her fear. She needed to pack some essentials in order to flee with Sarah. She couldn't afford to go into town with Matt, waste time there, when she could be making her escape. "I mean…what on earth would Sarah and I do in town for several hours? I can't be seen in public right now."

"True. But I'd planned on having you stay in my office."

"Oh, Matt, a sheriff's office is no place for a baby. Transporting her there would mean bringing all sorts of things for her comfort. Have you thought of that?"

"Well…no."

Beth listed everything she'd need to ensure Sarah's comfort. Diapers, several changes of clothes, blankets, change mat, her travel cot…

Matt raised his hands. "Okay, okay, you've made your point. But I think you'd be safer with me."

"We'll be fine here. The only people who know where I am are Lucy and Will. And they're not about to tell anyone." She touched his arm. "Seriously, Matt, we'll be fine here. I can call you if I don't feel safe."

SHE WAS RIGHT. If Hennessey suddenly turned up in town, asking questions… The bile rose in Matt's throat at the thought of Hennessey getting anywhere within a five-hundred-mile radius of Beth and Sarah.

Only when the bastards were behind bars would he feel okay about Beth's being seen around town, but at the moment it was probably too risky. If Hennessey or his henchmen did show up in Spruce Lake and happened to talk to someone who'd seen Beth driving into town with him, then she and Sarah would be in danger. Hennessey would have a photo of Beth gleaned from her license. It would be easy for someone to identify her from a photograph. He needed to keep them both hidden here.

"Okay, but promise you'll call me if you don't feel a hundred-percent safe."

Beth bristled. "Matt. Don't treat me like a child. I've been living on my own up here for months. I'll know if something doesn't feel right and of course I'd call you."

HE SIGHED AND NODDED, but the triumph she felt at manipulating him into leaving her at the cabin was a hollow one. How much more would she be deceiving him in the coming hours?

She almost wept at the thought of leaving Matt, but leave him she must—to protect him and Sarah. Her mind raced as she considered everything she had to accomplish if her plan was to work without a hitch. Her heart broke at the treachery of what she planned to do to a man who'd sacrificed so much for her.

She started making mental notes of all the supplies she needed to take with her on their journey to…wherever.

"Hey, you've gone all quiet on me again," he said and turned his head to plant a kiss on her palm.

Beth looked up and tried to force a smile. "Just tired. It's been quite a day." She wanted to tell Matt she loved him. But doing so would make leaving that much harder. She needed to keep her feelings to herself. And to preserve what energy she had. Until she found another safe refuge for Sarah and her, she knew she wouldn't be getting any sleep.

When Matt reached over and raised her chin, she wiped at the tear that escaped despite her best efforts.

Matt put his arm around her shoulders and kissed her hair. "Hey," he said, giving her shoulder a comforting squeeze. "When Hennessey and Morgan are behind bars, we can get on with our lives. You'll have a whole new family to love and care about you, and you'll make new friends here in Spruce Lake. When everything in L.A. is cleared up, you can contact your family and friends back there. You won't be cut off anymore."

Beth wished she shared Matt's confidence, but what he'd outlined for her future would never come to pass. She could see herself being a fugitive forever. Maybe she could move somewhere in New England. It seemed about as far removed from L.A. and Colorado as one could get. She could buy a new identity somewhere, another car. She *could* become invisible again. She had to believe that.

As if knowing she needed his strength right now, Matt pulled her into his arms and held her against him. She let the tears flow freely. Matt O'Malley encompassed everything she'd be leaving behind: security, companionship, passionate love. A future for her and Sarah. Acutely aware that she'd be breaking his heart as well as her own, Beth knew that leaving him was the only thing to do.

"Don't cry, sweetheart. I don't know how to deal with weeping women. Screaming babies are fine. But women who cry, particularly when it's the woman I love…well, it cuts me up." He dropped a gentle kiss on her lips.

THEY SLEPT SPOONED together. Matt held her against him so snugly, she could feel his heart beating and the evenness of his breathing.

This would be the last night they'd ever spend together and Beth wanted to weep all over again. She lay awake for hours, staring into the darkness, organizing what she had to do the following day.

When Sarah awoke during the night, she slipped out of Matt's arms and nursed her in the baby's room. Then she climbed back into bed, where she lay on her side, watching him as he slept. He'd rolled onto his back, the sheet pooled at his waist, and he'd flung one arm across his forehead. She was tempted to stay. So tempted. Never in her life would she be blessed enough to find a love like this again.

Chapter Sixteen

Beth was woken by a wet mouth closing over her nipple and came instantly awake. Matt was sitting on the side of the bed. Sarah lay beside her, suckling contentedly.

"I tried to wake you," he explained, "but you were dead to the world." He stretched out with Sarah between them and brushed a lock of hair from Beth's forehead. "She was screaming blue murder in your ear, and you didn't hear a thing."

Beth smiled bleakly. Already she could feel herself drawing back from him, erecting an emotional fence as though it could protect her from hurt.

"Sweetheart? What's wrong?" Matt moved closer.

Beth smiled and turned her head to kiss his hand. "Nothing. I guess I was having a bad dream." How many more lies would she need to tell before she could get away from here? When would it end—the agony of having to lie so blatantly to the man she loved? When would the heartache of never seeing him again cease?

"It must've been a bad dream. You look so sad. Want to talk about it?"

She shook her head and turned her attention to Sarah, making an effort to get her emotions under control, but that only made her teary. She bit down hard on her bottom lip, collected herself and said, "Could you please get me a glass of water, Matt?"

When he went to do her bidding, she muttered under her breath, "Get a grip on yourself. Otherwise he's going to get suspicious."

Sarah was alerted by her mother's voice and looked up at her, startled.

"I'm sorry, sweetie, for what I'm about to do. But it's for the best," she told her daughter, "and one day you'll know that."

When Sarah had finished nursing and fallen asleep, Beth brought her to her crib and went to take a shower. She washed her hair, then turned the shower to cold, trying to clear her mind and prepare for the day ahead. She endured the icy prickles for a moment, then flipped off the faucet and stepped out.

Joining Matt in the kitchen, she eyed the poached eggs he'd made for breakfast and felt her stomach revolt.

She watched him eat, barely able to pick at hers. Loathing herself, she knew she'd hurt Matt deeply and throw away her only chance of happiness, but it had to be done.

Beth insisted on clearing up the kitchen while he pressed his uniform. She gazed out to where she'd watched him splitting wood and hugged herself to stop trembling at the thought of their separation. Matt was a wonderful man. Passionate, caring, loving, honorable. Everything a woman could ever want. Was she wise to leave, after all? Couldn't they both just stay here forever, cocooned in the safety of the cabin? No, that wasn't possible, no matter how much she wanted it.

He returned a little while later, fully dressed, and she was taken aback by the contrast between her feelings for him now and her apprehension about him when she'd first met him.

How things had changed! In such a short time, Matt had gone from being the enemy to the love of her life.

She wrapped her arms around him and held on tight. "My handsome sheriff," she murmured, snuggling against his chest.

"If this is how you're going to see me off every morning, I'll never get to work." He kissed her deeply and Beth took pleasure in their last moments together.

"Matt, you have to go," she said, her voice breathless when he finally drew away.

"I know." He kissed her quickly. "I'll be back as soon as I can. We'll finish this then."

Beth stepped out into the winter sunshine. It was a glorious day. The sun reflected off the snow like millions of diamonds sprinkled all over the landscape. Somehow the beauty made her yearn even more for what she and Sarah would be missing.

"You're so lucky to have grown up in such a special place," she said and turned to face Matt, wanting, needing, her last sight of him so desperately. Her last moments with him.

Unable to talk, afraid her voice would crack with emotion, she clasped his hand and walked him to his vehicle, the snow crunching underfoot. This would be the final time she made this journey with him. The final time she'd see him, feel his protective warmth. His love.

At his vehicle, she cupped his cheek and said, "Goodbye, Matt."

Matt pulled her into his arms. "I'll be back as soon as I can, sweetheart," he murmured against her mouth, then kissed her.

Beth experienced the deepest pleasure in the feel of his lips, so warm and tender; his arms, so strong and protective; his embrace, so firm and loving. *This is madness,* she thought. *I'm crazy to be leaving a man like this. A love like this!* She clung to him, savoring their last moments together.

Matt eventually broke their embrace. "Darlin', if I don't get going now, I won't be able to leave."

She brushed his cheek, loving the feel of his freshly shaved face. "You have work to do. Go."

He tilted his head and studied her. "If I'd known what a slave driver you could be, I don't think I'd have proposed to you quite so readily," he teased. He gave her a melting kiss, then climbed into his truck.

"I'll see you in a couple of hours."

Beth forced cheerfulness to her voice. "Hurry home."

She watched him drive away, her heart breaking. She'd tried to put everything she felt for Matt into those last moments with him. All the love she felt for him, her gratitude and her regret for what she was about to do.

When Matt's vehicle disappeared from view, she walked back into the cabin, figuring out what essentials she needed to pack, her steps heavy with pain.

"Hi, Matt!" Ben Hansen greeted him as Matt strode in the door. "Glad you could make it today. I've gotta confess I wasn't looking forward to spending time with Mayor Farquar."

Matt checked through his mail as he walked toward his office. Nothing that couldn't wait till he'd seen Frank. He asked Ben for an update on the call he'd gotten from Hennessey the previous evening, then phoned a P.I. acquaintance in L.A. Sam Forester promised the utmost discretion and said he'd get back to him as soon as possible. Matt caught up on some paperwork while he waited for Forester to call.

Just over forty-five minutes later, Forester was back

on the line. "I've tracked down some dirt on these guys, Matt. Apparently the department's been suspicious of their activities for some time, even before the death of Marcus Jackson.

"When Jackson's wife disappeared, alarm bells started ringing. Internal Affairs got involved, but Hennessey heard about it and has been keeping a low profile. At the moment, he and Morgan are looking like model cops, but I don't think it'd take much to get the department to reopen their investigation. If you could get this woman to make a statement, that would go a long way. Has she got any physical evidence of their corruption?"

Matt hesitated. He didn't know Forester well enough to trust him with information about the safety-deposit-box key.

When he said he wasn't aware of any, Forester continued. "There was talk of drugs going missing from busts they worked on. The stuff's got to be out there somewhere. I just wondered if she'd told you anything about it."

Matt rubbed the back of his neck. "It's like I told you, Sam, she didn't have a clue what her husband was doing until Hennessey and Morgan turned up and threatened her. She disappeared, rather than risk losing her baby."

"And they claimed she'd gone on the run because she was wanted for questioning in her husband's death and a string of other felonies. All very convenient for them." He could hear the sigh in Forester's voice. "It'll come down to her word against theirs and, right now, it doesn't look good that she fled rather than going to the LAPD."

Matt tried to keep the frustration from his tone. "I explained to you why she couldn't do that."

"Yeah, yeah, I know." Forester's own frustration with the situation was evident. "Look, I'll keep digging, and if I turn up anything else, I'll get back to you. Take care."

Matt rested his elbows on the desk and rubbed his face. Maybe he should've trusted Forester with the information about the key. He'd wait and see what else the P.I. came up with and make his decision then. He was reluctant to reveal all his facts at once—not until he knew Beth was safe and Hennessey and his sidekicks were permanently behind bars.

He smiled with grim satisfaction. Prison wasn't a nice place for crooked cops.

BETH PACKED A SUITCASE, taking whatever she and Sarah needed and leaving the rest. She took the key from its hiding place and hid it in a bag of disposable diapers, then called Hank.

His number was busy, and when she tried again a few minutes later, it was still busy.

Hating having to call his cousin, Chuck, but needing to get away from the cabin as soon as possible, Beth punched in the number Hank had left for emergencies.

She'd never met Chuck but he seemed cheerful enough when he said, "I'll be up there as soon as I can, little lady," he said. "Just makin' a delivery."

Beth urged him to hurry, then hung up and cursed herself for not calling Hank the minute Matt had left the cabin. Still, she didn't expect him back until later this afternoon. There was plenty of time to make her escape and be long gone before Matt returned.

She sat at the kitchen table and carefully composed what to say in her farewell note, put it in an envelope and sealed it. As she placed it on the mantel, tears blurred her vision. *Don't lose it now. You have too much to do,* she told herself.

She fed and changed Sarah before Chuck arrived to collect them. "There we go, sweetie, all nice and dry," she said as she pulled on Sarah's sleeper and then another, warmer quilted one for traveling. Beth smiled at her daughter, all bundled up, the hood covering her head protectively.

The sound of a vehicle turning into her yard, its tires crunching on the snow outside her front door, set Beth's heart racing. This was it. She was leaving. She'd never see Matt O'Malley again.

She lifted Sarah into her carrier, fastened the safety harness and carried her to the living room. Placing it on the floor behind the sofa, she walked over to open the door.

Chapter Seventeen

Beth's smile froze as she looked up into Hennessey's face.

"Expecting someone else?" He grabbed her arm, pushing her backward into the cabin.

Beth made an effort not to lose her balance, determined to be strong, even though every bone in her body felt as though it had turned to water. Oh, Lord! Sarah was right there in her safety seat, behind the sofa! She stood her ground and shook off his hand. Hennessey's look of surprise at her sudden show of strength empowered her. "What are you doing here?" she asked, astonished that her voice didn't waver with fear.

"What d'you think, bitch? I've come for the key. Now, hand it over."

Beth was desperate to play for time. If she could stall Hennessey for a while, maybe Chuck would turn up, see what was going on and call for help.

"How did you find me?"

"Easy. Police computers can transmit all kinds of interesting information. Unfortunately I was on vacation and only got back yesterday. When I saw that a sheriff's office in Spruce Lake had made an inquiry about your driver's license, it didn't take long to track down the person who'd done it."

MATT'S MEETING with the mayor was thankfully short. The tension he'd felt earlier this morning had been somewhat alleviated by Sam Forester's news about Hennessey and Morgan being under investigation by Internal Affairs. At least it would make things easier for Beth if there was some preexisting suspicion about their activities.

He checked with the dispatcher and, learning there'd been no important calls for him, decided to head back to the cabin. Beth had acted strange this morning and it had been on his mind. He purchased roses at Mrs. Carmichael's—correction, Mrs. Farquar's—florist's shop, wanting to bring Beth a gift from his heart and thinking how good they'd look in their cozy cabin home.

Home. The word had such a satisfying ring to it. He couldn't wait to get back to the cabin.

"WHERE'S THE KEY?" Hennessey demanded, looming over Beth.

Mute with terror, she refused to cower beneath his hard glare.

Apparently, seeing that he was getting nowhere, Hennessey gripped the front of her jacket. "Where's the kid, then?"

The evil pulsing from his eyes made Beth's stomach turn. She was terrified at the thought of what he'd do to Sarah to get her to tell him where the key was.

"N-not here," she forced through icy lips.

Hennessey swore and pushed her away from him, scanning the small room.

Praying Sarah stayed snug and quiet in her car seat, Beth called on all her latent acting skills and said, "Sh-she died at birth."

"Liar!" Hennessey lashed out, his big hand striking her

across the face. She stumbled backward, holding her hand to her burning cheek.

"I know for a fact that she's alive." His eyes bored into Beth. "I've spoken to someone who's seen her."

The pain smarting in Beth's cheek was nothing to the pain that clenched her heart. She closed her eyes so he couldn't read the fear there as she asked, "Who?"

"Can't you guess?" Hennessey asked menacingly.

The image formed in Beth's mind. Matt! Had he betrayed her? *No!* Matt would *never* betray her.

Her mind tumbled with possibilities. Hank? The reward was so large…and he was a greedy man. Why had she trusted him? She didn't have time to ponder it now. She had to get Hennessey out of the cabin, away from Sarah, before he found her baby.

If she could lure them away from the cabin, Sarah might have a chance of survival. Someone would be coming by soon. If not the cabdriver, then Matt.

Forcing steel into her voice, she said, "The key isn't here. It's at the Spruce Lake Bank." Emboldened by his look of surprise, she told him, "They…they won't just hand it over to anyone. I'll have to go with you."

She moved toward the door, hoping Hennessey would follow, needing to get him out of the cabin and away from Sarah.

He seemed to consider, then nodded at Morgan and started toward her. "This better not be a trick," he said. "Remember we'll have our weapons at your back. One false move and you're dead. If you so much as blink and I don't like it, you're dead. Understand?"

Beth nodded.

"Let's go," he said, shoving Beth ahead of him.

Sarah chose that moment to moan softly in her sleep.

Hennessey froze midstep and spun toward the sound.

Beth's insides turned to water. "Leave her!" she cried. "She's got nothing to do with this!"

Ignoring her plea, Hennessey stepped around the end of the sofa. "Well, well, well, what have we here?" He sneered. "Oh, look! It's a *baby!*" he said, his voice dripping with sarcasm as he lifted Sarah out of her carrier and held her up in the air.

If Beth had been scared before, it was nothing compared to the terror she was feeling now. "Put her down!" she screamed and rushed at Hennessey.

Woken abruptly, Sarah began to wail.

Hennessey paid no attention to the baby's cries and fixed his gaze on Beth. "You lying bitch!" he spat and dropped Sarah back into her carrier. "You lied about her and you're lying about the key."

He backhanded Beth so hard she saw stars. Tears swam in her eyes but she refused to let them fall.

His eyes narrowed. "And you thought that if we'd gone to the bank, you would've been able to get away with something there!"

Hennessey reached down to Sarah and held the baby up again, taunting Beth, his eyes shining with cruelty. Then he threw Sarah in the air.

Beth screamed, beseeching him to leave her baby alone as Sarah's wails turned to screams of fear. Beth fell to her knees at Hennessey's feet. "Please, please put her down," she begged, tears streaming down her cheeks. "I'll do anything you want. Just please don't hurt her!"

"Where's the key?" Hennessey demanded, making a motion as if he'd throw the baby in the air again. Beth was terrified Sarah's neck would snap from the force and prayed that the quilted sleeper she wore offered some protection. "Tell me," he growled, "otherwise, next time, I won't catch her."

"Here!" Beth shouted, her voice shrill with terror as she grabbed for the bag containing Sarah's diapers and scrabbled through it, then sobbed with relief as her hand closed over the safety-deposit key. She held it up to him. "Take it! Just take it and leave us alone! I won't make any trouble for you, I promise. Please, please put my baby down," she begged, tears flowing freely. "She hasn't done anything to you. Punish me—not her."

Hennessey snatched the key from Beth's frozen fingers and dumped Sarah unceremoniously onto the sofa.

With a cry of relief, Beth reached for her baby, but Hennessey clutched her hair, hauling her back against him.

"Now you're going to pay for your lies," he snarled in her ear. He glanced up at Morgan. "Kill them. Kill them both," he snapped and released Beth. He tossed the key in the air and caught it as he strolled toward the door, leaving Morgan to dispose of them.

Beth bent down to pick up Sarah and felt Morgan's gun at her throat. Certain that Morgan had every intention of carrying out the order, she called on every bit of strength she had. She placed her crying baby back on the sofa in order to leave her hands free and to create two targets for Morgan instead of one. Perversely, Sarah stopped crying and looked around the room.

"Yeah, be the hero, Hennessey, why don't you?" She sneered at his back. "Leave the dirty work to your little henchman."

Hennessey turned toward her, gave a tiny salute, then continued toward the door.

That hadn't gone the way she'd hoped. She was hoping one of them would take umbrage at her taunt, particularly Morgan. She was in no doubt as to how long Morgan would live once Hennessey got his hands on the drugs and money.

She glanced at Morgan's gun. Thankfully it was still pointed at her and not Sarah. *I have to save Sarah.* But how? Everything in her screamed to rush at Morgan, try to wrest his weapon away from him. But she knew that course of action was fruitless. He was so much bigger and stronger; he'd overpower her in a second. The only weapon she had at her disposal was guile.

Morgan moved his pistol, aimed it at Sarah and flipped off the safety.

"No!" Beth shrieked, her voice hoarse with tension and abject fear.

Hennessey halted in the doorway. He turned slowly. "No?" He strode back into the room and stood over her. "I don't think you're in any position to call the shots around here." He gripped Beth's chin, lifting her face to his.

Out of the corner of her eye, she noticed that Morgan's weapon had come back around to her. Her heart was pounding, her palms sweating, but she made herself ignore her body's response and raised her chin, shaking off Hennessey's grip.

"That key will only open the box that contains all the incriminating papers," she said. "You know the ones, Hennessey? The lists of all the deals you and Marcus did over the years. You should be grateful I didn't send it to the LAPD. I'm sure they could've convicted you on that alone."

Beth felt her strength return as she watched Hennessey pale at her words. He couldn't know that she'd been too terrified to send it to the LAPD in case someone else in the department who was also corrupt had gotten hold of it. She turned away from Hennessey, her mind racing.

"Where's the other key, then?" Hennessey demanded.

"There *is* no key," she said, her smile triumphant.

Hennessey's eyes narrowed. "What're you saying?"

"I'm saying that if you touch one hair on my daughter's head, then those drugs and that money will rot in that L.A. bank vault forever."

Hennessey snorted. "Yeah, right!" He scowled at Morgan. "Kill 'em and let's get out of here. I'll get hold of the stuff somehow." He looked back at Beth and said, as he watched her carefully, "She's lying. I'll bet the other key's in the first box."

Beth crossed her arms and cocked her head on the side. "Jeez, Hennessey, you must think I'm as stupid as you are." She sneered, playing the bitch, enjoying the look of annoyance on Hennessey's face.

Enraged, Hennessey drew his weapon and pressed it against her cheek.

Beth detected the tremor in his hand.

Realizing he wasn't as much in control of the situation as he wanted to be encouraged her, firming her resolve. "Go on," she urged. "Kill me. But you'll never get your money."

Indecision flitted across Hennessey's features. "What are you doing?" he demanded.

Beth's eyes narrowed. "You think this is a game, Hennessey?" she almost screamed. "This is no game, you slimy bastard! This is life. *My* life. My *baby's* life. And I've had enough of you toying with it!"

She pushed the weapon away and stuck her face up close to his. Hennessey was too surprised by her action to react.

"You see, I should be thankful to you, Hennessey. You've forced me to toughen up over these past few months. I've had to be very cunning to keep one step ahead of you. I knew my life depended on you not getting access to that box, so I took precautions."

Beth wasn't the least bit fazed by Hennessey's growl

of frustration. Maybe if she played for time, the cab she'd ordered so long ago would show up. She didn't suppose Chuck would be able to help much, but at least his presence might even the odds somewhat.

"The other safety-deposit box can only be opened by my thumbprint."

Hennessey snorted and addressed Morgan. "Cut off her thumbs and then kill them." He glanced at his watch. "And hurry up about it."

Beth's stomach dropped at his words. What a stupid, naive fool she'd been to come up with the thumbprint routine! It had sprung to mind because they'd used it as a security measure on one of the homes she'd designed. Damn!

Morgan disappeared into the kitchen and came back with a meat cleaver.

An idea formed. "Just one little problem with that plan, Hennessey. The thumbprint security system is thermal sensitive. The sensors have to be able to detect body temperature within one degree of ninety-eight point six—otherwise, the whole vault shuts down, with you two clowns locked inside."

"She's lying!" Morgan yelled. "I've never heard of any such thing!"

Hennessey studied her for several long moments. "Maybe she is and maybe she isn't. I can't take that chance. We'll bring them with us. When we get to the bank, we'll cut off her thumb. That way, it'll still be warm enough for me to do what I need to do and get out of there. Then we can dispose of her and the kid."

No doubt Hennessey intended to drive back to California. It would be too risky to take them on a plane, but if they brought Sarah with them, the baby wouldn't be safe. A dozen hideous scenarios filled her mind at the fate that might befall Sarah if Hennessey killed her but not Sarah....

Once he recognized her deception and found the second key in the safety-deposit box, he'd kill her; Beth was in no doubt of that. Unless she could get away from him before they reached L.A., she would die. And when Hennessey realized she'd played him for a fool, it wouldn't be a quick death, either.

Her only chance now was to escape from Hennessey somewhere between here and L.A. But if she had the added burden of Sarah, she'd never be able to accomplish that.

"Leave my daughter here. Otherwise, the deal's off." She snatched the cleaver from Morgan's grip. Bracing her hand on the stone mantel, she held the cleaver above her thumb. "You leave her or I cut it off right now," she threatened. "And there's no way you're going to be able to heat it back up to the correct temperature again!" The cleaver trembled in her grip.

Hennessey paused as though undecided.

"Leave the kid," he finally snapped.

Beth released a sigh of relief and dropped the cleaver as Hennessey grasped the back of her hair and dragged her toward the door.

All the fight gone out of her. Beth stumbled as she looked back at Sarah, her tiny arms waving in the air. "Sarah!" she cried, trying to imprint the last image of her beautiful daughter on her mind.

At least they were leaving her precious baby behind. At least she had a chance! Matt would find her when he returned. Sarah would be safe with Matt.

A sob of anguish escaped her throat. What would happen to her little girl, left alone in the world? How desperately she wanted to keep her baby with her.

Morgan was about to close the door when he said, "If

we leave the kid, that sheriff's gonna know we've got the woman. If we take both of 'em, he might figure she's taken off again."

Hennessey halted in his tracks and spun around to Morgan. "You're right. Good thinking—for once," he snapped at his partner. "Get the kid!"

"No!" Beth screamed as she struggled out of Hennessey's grasp and ran toward the cabin. How stupid could she have been!

She raced into the living room but Morgan had already picked up Sarah. Not wanting to give him an opportunity to repeat Hennessey's cruel action of throwing Sarah into the air, she stopped and held up her hands in front of her. She had to go along with them. Play for time.

Morgan moved toward the door, the baby struggling in his awkward hold.

Thinking quickly, she said, "Sarah gets carsick. If you put her in her car seat, she won't throw up on you."

Morgan didn't need any more prompting than that. He handed the baby to Beth.

A warm wave of relief swept over her. She held the baby against her heart and cooed to her. Sarah quieted immediately. "That's my girl," Beth murmured softly, tears pouring down her cheeks. "Everything's all right. Mommy's here." Whatever happened in the next few minutes or hours, she had to ensure Sarah was safe. As much as she wanted to hold Sarah close and protect her from Hennessey, Beth knew her baby would be safer in her carrier.

She fastened Sarah into it, making sure she was secure, and wished she had the base it fit into for safe vehicular transport. Lord only knew what sort of roads they'd be driving on to escape detection once Matt realized she'd been taken by Hennessey. And if they had an accident… Beth squeezed her eyes shut at the prospect of Sarah becoming a human missile if the vehicle crashed.

Closely following that horrifying thought was the realization Matt might believe she'd run away. After all, she'd left the note.... She glanced at where it lay on the mantel.

"Come on!" Hennessey lunged at Sarah's carrier, trying to wrest it from Beth's grasp.

She held on, refusing to relinquish her daughter.

With a groan of frustration, Hennessey dragged both of them out the door behind him.

At the vehicle, he pushed Beth roughly into the backseat. "Don't forget to wear your seat belt," he taunted her in a singsong voice, then slammed the door, strode around the car and got in the other side.

In the absence of any suitable restraining device for Sarah's carrier, Beth decided the safest place for her daughter was on the floor of the vehicle. She wedged the carrier between the rear of the driver's seat and the backseat and prayed it would offer sufficient protection.

Hennessey sneered at her makeshift safety measures. "You'll both be dead soon enough." As he lifted his hand, Beth saw the sun sparkle against the metal of Hennessey's service revolver. Then everything went black.

MATT HEADED OUT of Spruce Lake and turned off to Blue Spruce Drive, narrowly missing a black Chevy Blazer as it made a sharp turn at the intersection, the driver having failed to brake sufficiently after his descent down the steep mountain road.

Matt considered turning around and giving the guy a warning, but let it go. He wanted to get back to Beth.

But when he pulled up at the cabin, Matt sensed something wasn't right. He climbed down from his vehicle and looked around. A thin stream of smoke issued from the chimney. He let himself in through the front door, dropped the roses on the coffee table and hurried into the bedroom to find Beth.

She wasn't there. Neither was Sarah.

On shaky legs he strode to the fireplace, where Beth had concealed the key, and pried the mortar away, half knowing it wouldn't be there.

He cursed long and loud. She'd fooled him. Sucked him in, let him fall in love with her, with Sarah, let him make plans for their future—tricked him completely. And now she'd taken off with Sarah and the key—presumably to claim whatever the box held. With him gone, she'd felt safe enough to come out of hiding and head back to L.A. He didn't even know what bank the safety-deposit key was for.

He should've guessed something was up from her strange behavior this morning. And in spite of all his declarations of love, she'd never once said those three little words to him. Instead, she'd played him for the lovesick fool he was. Damn her!

Anguish twisting through him. He wondered, *How had she gotten away from the cabin?*

A vehicle pulled up outside, tooting its horn. He raced to the door and pulled it open so hard it nearly came off its hinges. "Beth!"

"Whoa, there, Matt!" Chuck Farquar yelled in warning as Matt barreled into him.

"Where is she?" Matt bellowed, pushing him aside and striding to his vehicle.

Chuck trotted back to his cab. "Who?"

"Beth! The woman who lives here! She's gone! Where the hell is she?"

Chuck stroked his jaw in the slow, lazy, considering way

that was typical of Chuck's entire family and drove Matt to distraction. "Well, seeing's as I was s'posed to pick her up here, I was hopin' you could tell me."

Matt grabbed him by the collar. "What're you saying?"

Chuck tried to free himself from Matt's fingers. "She booked a cab a while ago, but I was busy. She seemed to want to get away from here fast, though." He scratched his head. "Maybe she hitched a ride with someone goin' down the drive?"

Matt released his grip on Chuck. Something wasn't right here. He could feel it deep in his marrow. Beth was way too cautious to ever accept a ride from a stranger.

"Y'know," Chuck was saying. "Hank was tellin' me—"

Frantic, Matt rounded on him. "Shut up about Hank! I'm sick and tired of that fool cousin of yours and his gossiping." He paced the ground between the cabin and the cab and tore at his hair. "Where the *hell* can she be?"

"It's only that there was some men from outta town askin' about a woman this mornin' down at the feed store."

Matt felt his bowels turn to water. He stopped his pacing and glared at Chuck. "What did you say?"

"I said that a couple men from outta town were askin' about the woman who drove that little red sports car off the road." He scratched his head as though he had all the time in the world to impart his news.

Matt cursed and grabbed Chuck's shirtfront. "What did you tell them?" he demanded.

Chuck tried to swallow. "Easy, Matt. Yer squeezin' the life outta me!"

"Tell me!"

"Well...like I was sayin', I knew Hank towed the car,

'cause he told me he did. And he kinda hinted he knew more about her than everyone else around here did. But—"

"Shut up and get to the point! What did *you* tell them?"

Chuck shrugged and eased his fingers into his collar. "I told 'em that Hank towed her car and so he might know where she lived. They gave me two hundred dollars to tell 'em where to find Hank."

Matt let go of Chuck's collar and staggered away. He'd been right. Hank's gossiping was going to get someone in trouble one day. Only he hadn't guessed it could be as bad as this.

"That woman lives here, and your idiot cousin and his big mouth have led to her being abducted, along with her daughter."

He pulled out his phone and punched in Hank's number while Chuck mumbled his excuses.

"I thought it was interestin' gettin' a call to this address, since Hank owns the cabin." Chuck tilted his head. "Kinda makes sense, don't it?"

When Hank came on the line, Matt was short and to the point. "How long ago were those men looking for Beth?"

"Well, let's see now—" Hank drawled, but Matt cut him off.

"How long, dammit?"

"'Bout…forty-five minutes, I guess."

"What were they driving?"

"A black Blazer. Say, Matt—"

Matt cut the connection. *The black Blazer!*

He climbed into his vehicle and started it, picked up the radio mike and called his office as he peeled out of the driveway, leaving Chuck standing outside the cabin, openmouthed. "Be on the lookout for a black Blazer, possibly heading north on Silver Springs Highway. You are to trail but not approach."

Matt spun the wheel as he hit the bottom of Blue Spruce Drive and called the state highway patrol and demanded to be put through to the local captain. Cutting into the other man's welcoming chitchat, he explained the situation quickly.

"These guys are cops," he said. "They're to be approached with extreme caution. There's a possibility that if you stop them, they'll use the woman and child as hostages."

"Gotcha, Matt," the captain said. "We're on it."

Matt ended the call, hit his siren and pressed his accelerator to the floor.

He sped through Spruce Lake, heedless of the posted speeds, almost uncaring of what lay in his way. His one objective was to get to Beth and Sarah—while they were still alive.

Matt's cell rang. "Yeah?" he growled as he fought the wheel on the slippery road.

"Matt. It's Sam Forester. Bad news, I'm afraid."

"If you're calling to tell me Hennessey and Morgan caught a flight out here, I already know." He cursed the fact that Forester hadn't called him half an hour ago. Then he would've at least had a chance of getting to the cabin in time to save Beth and Sarah.

He said a hurried goodbye when his radio crackled. "We've got them, Matt," the state patrol captain told him. "They're in Silver Springs, but I think they'd gotten lost. That turnoff sign to the interstate has snow piled up over it where they're clearing the roads. They're driving around in circles."

Relief flooded Matt. They'd found them! Now came the

tricky part. "Okay. Keep an eye on them, but please—don't approach. Can you see any other passengers?"

"There's a driver and the only passenger I can see, another male, is sitting in the backseat. I can't see anyone else. We're setting up spike strips at the top of the ramp onto the interstate."

Matt cursed. "If you stop them, they'll go to ground, taking the woman and baby as hostages."

"Relax, Matt. It's that blind bend. They won't know it's there until they hit it. I suggest you tell your men to back off so these two don't get suspicious."

"He's stopping at the gas station," one of his deputies reported. "Asking directions by the look of it."

"Just keep cruising by." He had to get there in time. He'd *promised* he'd keep them safe.

Damn the highway patrol! The Blazer could come out of that blind corner at top speed and hit those spikes so hard it could roll over. If Beth and Sarah weren't properly secured, their lives would be at risk. Provided Hennessey hadn't disposed of them already.

Matt fought the suffocating notion. He had to believe they were in the Blazer and belted in safely.

The town limits signpost for Silver Springs flew past his window. As he wove his truck through the town's traffic and toward the entry ramp to the interstate, he flipped off his siren.

"He's pulling out of the gas station, Matt," the deputy said. "He's heading for the interstate and I just saw a woman's face at the rear window. She sat up for only a second, then the guy in the backseat pushed her down again."

Beth was alive! "Everybody, *back off.* I don't want this guy getting panicky. They'll be armed and won't hesitate to use their weapons if they think they've been cornered."

Matt's heart pounded as the Blazer came into view ahead

of him. When it made a left onto the street leading to the interstate on-ramp, he followed, turning the corner against the lights, then trailed the Blazer at a discreet distance as it reached the ramp. "Go on, go on," he muttered, "Take it. *Take* it."

Despite his earlier opinion, Matt decided that forcing the Blazer onto the interstate was probably the best solution, regardless of the inherent dangers to Beth and Sarah. They needed to get Hennessey and his accomplice when they were least expecting an ambush. If Hennessey stopped in town and made a run for it, people could get hurt in a possible shoot-out or siege. Sieges rarely ended well.

The Blazer's brake lights flashed on and off as though the driver was uncertain about what to do. "Damn!" Matt cursed his impatience and backed off a little, watching carefully. Although he drove an unmarked vehicle, he felt as conspicuous as a snowplow charging through the streets.

As the traffic slowed to a crawl, Matt resisted the urge to close up the space between him and the Blazer. He could see the town police up ahead, directing traffic away from the on-ramp in order to keep it clear. To the Blazer driver it would look like a roadblock, as if the cops were stopping people to question them. The next few minutes were critical. Would the Blazer's driver fall for the bait and take the on-ramp or take his chances with the roadblock?

Matt's hands twitched with pent-up energy as he waited. Sure enough, a puff of dark smoke issued from the exhaust as the driver floored the Blazer, spun the wheel and took the interstate on-ramp.

Matt slammed his gear lever into Second, stepped on the accelerator and followed the Blazer onto the ramp. His speedometer shot past fifty-five as it twisted around in a corkscrew.

As he neared the top of the ramp where it straightened out onto the interstate, he could see the Blazer hitting the spike strips and the tires deflating.

Matt slowed to allow the state troopers to pull the spike strips aside to let him pass. The Blazer's driver wasn't giving up, though, and the vehicle continued along the interstate.

"Pull over, damn you!" Matt shouted as he followed the Blazer, which was now riding on its rims, tires shredding, rubber flying everywhere.

The stench of burned rubber, police sirens and the screech of the Blazer's rims as they scraped along the tarmac, filled the air.

The driver obviously had no intention of stopping, so Matt eased up behind him to perform a pursuit intervention technique, tapping his front bumper to the outside corner of the Blazer. When it spun out and came to rest facing the opposite direction, Matt hit his brakes and leaped out of his car, ignoring the cries of, "Get back!" from the state troopers, their weapons drawn.

Ignoring the driver hunched over the wheel, he ran to the Blazer's right-side rear passenger door and wrenched it open.

Beth lay motionless, her head slumped against the seat.

Two dark eyes glared at Matt from the other passenger seat. Hennessey's weapon was pointed straight at him. "You move, you're dead," he threatened, leaning toward him.

Matt reacted the only way he could. He'd promised to protect Beth, to keep her safe, and he'd failed. He wouldn't fail her again.

Lightning-fast, his closed fist connected with the other man's nose, smashing it.

Hennessey screamed with pain as blood poured from his nose.

"You bastard!" Hennessey swore. He grabbed Beth by the hair and reached for the door handle beside him.

There was no way Matt was letting Hennessey drag her out of the vehicle with him. He lashed out and struck the other man again and Hennessey collapsed against the seat, unconscious.

Beth moaned and lifted her head. With infinite gentleness, Matt caught her to him and unfastened her seat belt. "Easy, sweetheart. Easy. It's all over. Everything's going to be fine now," he assured her as a trooper pulled open the door on Hennessey's side and dragged the unconscious man onto the ground. Other troopers crowded around his inert body, their weapons aimed at him.

Sarah's cry of indignation from her carrier on the floor between Beth's legs was about the sweetest sound Matt had ever heard. He bent to lift Beth's leg aside, to check on Sarah.

"Aaaah!" she cried, tears of pain filling her eyes.

Matt got a flashlight from one of the troopers and shone it to the floor. Beth's leg was caught awkwardly between Sarah's carrier and the front seat.

The vehicle was swarming with police and paramedics, attending to the driver and Hennessey, but none of them could get past Matt. He was blocking the way, protecting Beth and Sarah.

"I-is Sarah all right?" Beth's voice held alarm now that she was becoming conscious of what was going on.

Matt reached carefully between her legs and gently withdrew Sarah from the safety harness that held her so securely in the baby carrier. "There, there, sweetie," he cooed. "Matt's here."

He placed a kiss on Sarah's cheek, then handed her to Beth.

"I'm sorry. I'm so sorry. I failed you both." Matt's voice broke as he wrapped his arms around them and buried his face against Beth's neck.

Beth clasped his shoulder with her free arm. "Shhh," she soothed and kissed him. "We're fine, my darling. We're together. Everything's going to be okay."

Matt leaned back to look into her eyes and saw the love reflected there. Then they clouded over with pain. "I love you," she whispered and passed out.

Epilogue

Six weeks later

Sitting on the sofa in Two Elk's living room, Beth's heart was filled with love as she watched the man she loved chatting with his nieces and nephew. Sarah was awake, lying in his arms and soaking up all the attention. She was a placid, happy baby who obviously adored her adoptive father.

When Matt glanced over at Beth and winked, she experienced the same warm flutter of anticipation that she'd felt whenever Matt's eyes met hers these past weeks.

They'd exchanged their wedding vows that morning, followed by a combined wedding reception and a baptismal party for Sarah. Will and Becky had stood with them as best man and matron of honor and were also Sarah's godparents.

And now the afternoon was winding down. Many of the guests had left, but Louella, Mayor Frank Farquar's pet pig, and her canine companion, Charles, were snoring on the sofa opposite Beth, and Frank didn't want to disturb them.

His delightful wife, Edna, had rolled her eyes and smiled indulgently at her eccentric husband. Edna had supplied the flowers for the occasion and their scent pervaded the ranch house.

The broken ankle Beth had sustained when Matt apprehended Hennessey and Morgan was a small price to pay for her freedom.

Matt's nieces and Will and Becky's son, Nicolas, had come to visit Beth during her convalescence, clutching tiny bouquets of flowers or get-well cards they'd made. She'd been touched by their thoughtfulness and the way they'd fought over Sarah and treated her as though she was already one of the family.

During the past six weeks, Beth had met many of the residents of Spruce Lake and gotten to know their idiosyncrasies. Miss Patterson had presented them with a cherished wedding gift—a painting of the cabin on Blue Spruce Drive. It would be their home until their new house was built on the ranchland Will was developing. Beth had drafted complete plans and they were being considered by the town planning department. She couldn't wait to fill the home with brothers and sisters for Sarah.

Nicolas had been generously rewarded by Matt for finding his cat, Wendy. She was presently terrorizing Nick's Scottish terrier, Dugald, and Miss Patterson's toy poodle, Louis, by suddenly appearing in front of them, hissing and then racing off with two small barking dogs in hot pursuit, while Louella and Charles slept on.

The house had been full of animals, children and pandemonium all day, and Beth had loved every minute of it.

MATT'S PARENTS HAD returned from their vacation and she'd fallen in love with them immediately. Matt's dad was tall and quiet, with the same inner strength and integrity he'd passed on to his son. Matt's mom was an angel, fairhaired and funny and full of boundless love. Beth couldn't hope for Sarah to have been loved and wanted any more than she was by these people. They were a wonderful family. The kind of family she'd always dreamed of having.

As a special surprise, Matt had arranged for her mother and grandmother to fly out from L.A. the day after he'd arrested Hennessey and Morgan. With Beth's statement and the evidence contained in the notebook, the pair were facing a host of charges in two states. Charges that would see them behind bars for the rest of their lives.

Grandma Elizabeth fit right in with the O'Malleys and had been invited to stay as long as she wanted. Beth had heard rumors, so far unconfirmed, that her grandmother was thinking of buying one of the Victorian homes that Will and Jack were renovating on Main Street. She and Edna Farquar shared a love of flowers and had already become firm friends.

Beth's mother had visited briefly, flitted around, bestowed her blessings and gone off to join a desert retreat in Arizona for a month. She hadn't come back in time for the wedding. It seemed nothing had changed there. Marcus's parents, when told of their son's corruption, had refused to believe any of the charges. They'd threatened to sue for custody of Sarah but given the circumstances didn't stand a chance. They'd since broken off all communication and Beth was glad of it.

Matt smiled over at her again with that secret smile of lovers. The one that said, *Just wait until we get home.*

Beth felt the flush creeping up her face. She glanced around, hoping the other occupants of the living room hadn't noticed.

Matt relinquished Sarah to her namesake's care and joined Beth on the sofa, lifting her gently to nestle in his lap.

She turned in his arms, laid her palm against his cheek and said, "Have I told you that I'm sorry for treating you so badly and for not trusting you? For not allowing myself to love you the way you deserved to be loved?"

"But you do now?"

"Oh, yes," she said and kissed him. "Heart and mind, body and soul." She smiled secretively. "And I aim to prove it."

"Tonight?" he asked hoarsely.

Beth rested her hands on his broad chest and looked deep into his eyes. "Yes, tonight, my love," she whispered and snuggled closer into Matt's protective embrace.

* * * * *

Return to Spruce Lake, Colorado,
soon for Luke O'Malley's story.
Watch for COLORADO COWBOY
in October, wherever
Harlequin Books are sold.

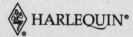
HARLEQUIN®

American ★ Romance®

COMING NEXT MONTH

Available July 13, 2010

#1313 THE LAWMAN'S LITTLE SURPRISE
Babies & Bachelors USA
Roxann Delaney

#1314 DEXTER: HONORABLE COWBOY
The Codys: The First Family of Rodeo
Marin Thomas

#1315 A MOM FOR CALLIE
Laura Bradford

#1316 FIREFIGHTER DADDY
Fatherhood
Lee McKenzie

HARLEQUIN®

A Romance

FOR EVERY MOOD™

Spotlight on

— Heart & Home —

Heartwarming romances
where love can happen
right when you least expect it.

See the next page to enjoy a sneak peek
from Silhouette Special Edition®,
a Heart and Home series.

*Introducing McFARLANE'S PERFECT BRIDE
by USA TODAY bestselling author Christine Rimmer,
from Silhouette Special Edition®.*

Entranced. Captivated. Enchanted.

Connor sat across the table from Tori Jones and couldn't help thinking that those words exactly described what effect the small-town schoolteacher had on him. He might as well stop trying to tell himself he wasn't interested. He was powerfully drawn to her.

Clearly, he should have dated more when he was younger.

There had been a couple of other women since Jennifer had walked out on him. But he had never been entranced. Or captivated. Or enchanted.

Until now.

He wanted her—*her,* Tori Jones, in particular. Not just someone suitably attractive and well-bred, as Jennifer had been. Not just someone sophisticated, sexually exciting and discreet, which pretty much described the two women he'd dated after his marriage crashed and burned.

It came to him that he…he *liked* this woman. And that was new to him. He liked her quick wit, her wisdom and her big heart. He liked the passion in her voice when she talked about things she believed in.

He liked *her.* And suddenly it mattered all out of proportion that she might like him, too.

Was he losing it? He couldn't help but wonder. Was he cracking under the strain—of the soured economy, the McFarlane House setbacks, his divorce, the scary changes in his son? Of the changes he'd decided he needed to make in his life and himself?

Strangely, right then, on his first date with Tori Jones, he didn't care if he just might be going over the edge. He was having a great time—having *fun,* of all things—and he didn't want it to end.

Is Connor finally able to admit his feelings to Tori, and are they reciprocated?
Find out in McFarlane's Perfect Bride
by USA TODAY *bestselling author Christine Rimmer.*
Available July 2010,
only from Silhouette Special Edition®.

Silhouette *Desire*

USA TODAY bestselling author

MAUREEN CHILD

brings you the first
of a six-book miniseries—

Dynasties: The Jarrods

Book one:

CLAIMING HER BILLION-DOLLAR BIRTHRIGHT

Erica Prentice has set out to claim
her billion-dollar inheritance
and the man she loves.

Available in July
wherever you buy books.

Always Powerful, Passionate and Provocative.